THIS BOOK BELONGS TO:

....

AUTUMN
PUBLISHING

Published in 2022
First published in the UK by Autumn Publishing
An imprint of Igloo Books Ltd
Cottage Farm, NN6 0BJ, UK
Owned by Bonnier Books
Sveavägen 56, Stockholm, Sweden
www.igloobooks.com

© 2022 MARVEL

0922 001
2 4 6 8 10 9 7 5 3 1
ISBN 978-1-80108-268-6

Designed by Aimee Swallow
Edited by Nicholas Oliver

Printed and manufactured in China

MARVEL
ULTIMATE STORYBOOK

AUTUMN
PUBLISHING

Contents

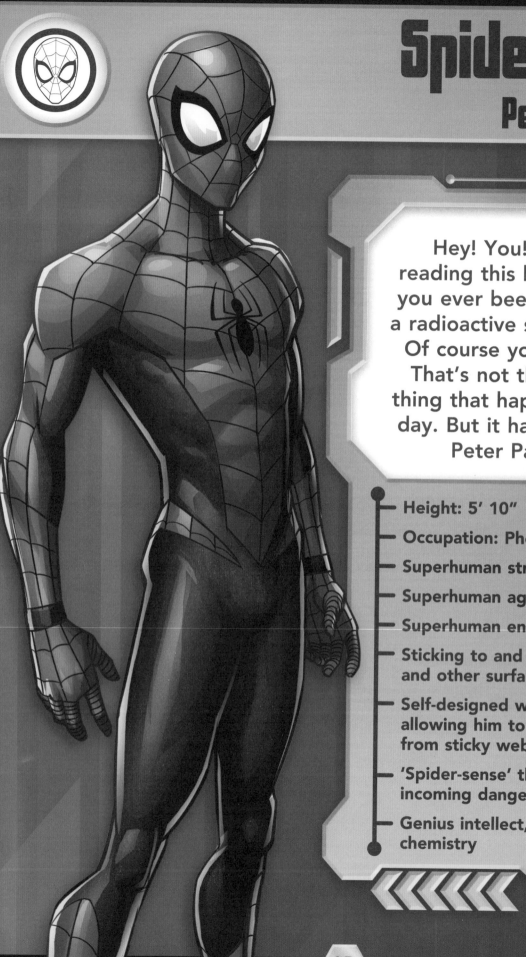

Spider-Man
Peter Parker

Hey! You! Person reading this book! Have you ever been bitten by a radioactive spider? No? Of course you haven't! That's not the sort of thing that happens every day. But it happened to Peter Parker!

- Height: 5' 10"
- Occupation: Photographer
- Superhuman strength
- Superhuman agility
- Superhuman endurance
- Sticking to and climbing walls and other surfaces
- Self-designed web-shooters, allowing him to fire and swing from sticky webs
- 'Spider-sense' that warns of incoming danger
- Genius intellect, specialising in chemistry

Friendly Neighbourhood Super Hero

Peter Parker was a lot like many teenagers his age. Peter liked being independent and figuring things out on his own. He loved to explore new places or just hang out in his hometown of New York City.

Peter lived in a house in Queens, New York, with his Aunt May.

She raised Peter as if he were her own son. She was very nurturing and made sure he had everything he needed. Before his Uncle Ben passed away, he told

Peter he could become whoever he wanted to be and to always remember that 'with great power comes great responsibility'.

Peter went to Midtown High School and was very focused on getting good grades.

He studied hard and achieved straight As. What made him such a good student was the fact that he loved learning.

Science was Peter's favourite subject, and he was one of the smartest students in class! He enjoyed performing science experiments and showing off his discoveries to his teacher.

After school, Peter worked at the *Daily Bugle* as a photographer. He had a knack for taking pictures – that is, when his boss wasn't yelling at him for more shots of a certain red-and-blue-clad Super Hero!

J. Jonah Jameson had a reputation for being tough-as-nails. He was also Peter's boss. Naturally Peter wanted to do a good job and keep Jameson happy. However, Jameson's constant demands for pictures of Spider-Man created a bit of a problem.

Peter had a secret that he couldn't tell anyone – not his Aunt May, and certainly not Jameson. It was the reason why getting certain photos was tricky. It was why he suddenly disappeared whenever danger loomed. It was also why he never seemed to get enough sleep.

Peter secretly *was* Spider-Man!

He became Spider-Man when a radioactive spider bit him during a school field trip to a science lab.

Suddenly, Peter discovered he could do extraordinary things like climb walls and jump high, just like a spider! He also used his knowledge of science to make special web-shooters. He practised a lot until his webs went in exactly the direction he wanted and he could swing on them.

Peter had to keep his identity a secret. That's where a little creativity came in. It took several tries and the use of Aunt May's sewing kit, but finally Peter made himself a spider-suit and mask fit for a Super Hero! Now he could go out into the city, scale walls and shoot webs without anyone knowing it was him.

Eventually, with time and a lot of practice, Peter learnt how to master all of his skills.

Besides web-shooting and wall-clinging, he also had super-strength. That strength, combined with Peter's courage and his other powers, gave him the ability to help those in trouble. He made it his mission to protect the people in his neighbourhood. That's how he earned the nickname 'your friendly neighbourhood Spider-Man'.

Peter also had the power of spider-sense. A strong tingling sensation would alert him to villains and danger.

There was one super villain who was Spider-Man's greatest enemy: Venom! Venom could shapeshift and use his special suit to make weapons. He could also mimic Spider-Man's abilities. With his super-strength and menacing fangs, Venom was extremely dangerous!

BOOM! Venom was wreaking

havoc in Times Square. Spidey swooped down and fired his webs, but the super villain blocked him shot for shot.

"Is that the best you can do?" snarled Venom.

As Venom charged towards him, Spider-Man remembered one of Venom's weaknesses. Thinking quickly, Spider-Man blasted webs at several nearby cars, setting off loud, blaring car alarms.

The noise caught Venom off guard, giving Spider-Man just enough time to ensnare him in thick webbing and defeat him.

"What was that, Venom? I can't hear you!" smirked Spider-Man.

The demands of being a Super Hero kept the web-slinger on his toes. Just days later, he surprised the Looter as the villain was trying to rob a bank.

THWIP! THWIP! Spider-Man shot a series of webs that pinned the Looter down. Then he returned the stolen money to the authorities.

Spider-Man hoped the day would soon come when the world would be free of criminals and villains. Until then, he swung through the city on patrol, ready for his spider-sense to alert him to danger, poised to jump in and help wherever he could.

When he wasn't fighting crime, Peter still went to school. He smiled secretly whenever he heard people talking about Spider-Man's latest act of bravery.

It wasn't easy living a double life, but he had to keep his identity a secret.

When times were tough, he reminded himself that he'd been given his powers for a reason. As long as there were villains, he had an important job to do.

Peter Parker was still a lot like other teenagers his age, except for one thing…

He was the Amazing Spider-Man!

BOOM! A tremendous noise echoed through the streets of New York City. The ground shook so hard that car alarms went off and stray cats hid under bins.

Spider-Man looked down – his spider-sense on high alert – and spotted Iron Man battling a strange feathery villain. It was Spidey's old enemy – Vulture! Spider-Man swooped in to help. Working together, Spider-Man and Iron Man had Vulture defeated in no time.

"Thanks, kid," said Iron Man. "We make a pretty great team."

"You're welcome, Mr Stark," replied Spidey. Iron Man, billionaire Tony Stark, was a big deal.

"Please, Mr Stark was my father," joked Iron Man. He put his arm around Spider-Man. "You know, some of the greatest victories have been won by heroes working as a team. Like the time Cap, Falcon and I teamed up to fight Hydra, or when A.I.M. were taken down by Widow and Hawkeye. Every hero has certain strengths and weaknesses."

"Well, I usually work alone," explained Spider-Man. "I don't think I've earned my place among the real heroes yet."

"There's no shame in needing a little help," said Iron Man, smiling. "See ya around, kid."

As Iron Man rocketed away, Spider-Man began to think about how cool all the other heroes were, and how badly he wanted to prove himself.

That gave him an idea. What if he threw a party for them? They deserved it – they saved the world every day, after all.

That night, Spider-Man went home and took off his suit. At home, he could be just regular old Peter Parker. The more Peter thought about it, the better he liked the idea of throwing a party for the other heroes. *A great party would definitely impress the Avengers!* he thought.

Peter immediately got to work.

He wrote invitations to all the Super Heroes he could think of. He knew Central Park would be the perfect place to host the party. It was going to be awesome!

Peter's invitations made their way to every famous Super Hero in the world.

But one invitation made its way – entirely by accident – through a rogue wormhole right into the hands of Thanos, the cosmic super villain.

"All of Earth's Mightiest Heroes in one place?" said Thanos, reading the invitation. "This is my chance to destroy them all in one single blow!"

The party started out great. Peter served delicious cupcakes and even made a Mysterio-shaped piñata. Everyone showed up and brought things for the party! Hulk had baked a green cake. Doctor Strange put on a dazzling light show. Hawkeye set up an indestructible game of whack-a-mole, and laughed as a frustrated Thor whacked away at it with his hammer, Mjolnir. Everyone was having a great time!

Suddenly, the sky turned dark and stormy. Lightning cracked against the grey clouds.

"We're under attack!" shouted Captain America, as thousands of alien cyborgs started pouring through a portal.

"It's the Chitauri!" yelled Black Widow.

Every hero leapt into action.

The party fell into chaos as the world's greatest heroes battled the galaxy's fiercest enemy. Spidey watched in awe. Every hero was needed in this fight – and that included him! He threw himself into battle, firing webs at lightning speed.

The greatest Super Heroes in the world, including Spider-Man, fought long and hard. Soon, the tide of the battle had turned. Fallen cyborgs littered the ground.

One by one, the heroes were defeated.

Suddenly, Spider-Man remembered what Iron Man had told him: *Some of the greatest victories have been won by heroes working as a team.*

That's what they needed! None of them could defeat Thanos alone. But if they all teamed up…

"Everybody!" cried Spidey. "We need to work together!"

With Spider-Man leading the assault, the heroes all fell in. Each hero brought their greatest strengths to the fight.

But then, with a mighty CRACK, the sky split open and Thanos appeared. Spider-Man's heart sank. The Chitauri were bad news, but Thanos was way worse. The world was really in trouble now.

"I've got him!" cried Captain America, but Thanos saw Cap charging and threw him into a tree. Black Panther leapt at Thanos, kicking powerfully, but the blow bounced right off Thanos's chest. Doctor Strange's magic couldn't contain the massive villain, and even Hawkeye's sharpest arrow bounced harmlessly away.

"We need to reverse the portal," realised Spidey. "Come on, heroes, let's knock this tough Titan into oblivion!"

When the Super Heroes worked as one, they were an invincible army!

In the fiercest battle Central Park had ever seen, Spider-Man and his friends banished Thanos to a far-off dimension in the multiverse. The world was safe.

"Teaching me my own words of wisdom?" asked Iron Man, slinging a metal-clad arm around Spider-Man's shoulders. "You're a pretty smart kid."

"Maybe even smarter than you," laughed Spidey.

"Hey, now, don't get crazy," replied Iron Man.

Spider-Man had finally won his place among the greatest heroes of the age!

"For Asgard!" cried Thor. A blast of lightning ripped through the sky towards his enemy, Enchantress, who blocked it with an energy shield.

"Love to chat, but I have unfinished business on Earth," cooed the sorceress.

"Heimdall will not let you pass," replied Thor.

"Good thing I have my own way of getting around."

With a snap of her fingers, Enchantress disappeared through a portal.

"Heimdall, open the bridge!" cried Thor. He had no idea how the Enchantress had escaped her holding cell or what she planned to do on Earth, but he knew he had to stop her.

Enchantress was a powerful sorceress, and even Thor was going to need some help.

It was time for the Avengers to assemble.

Nearby, in the cosmos, the Guardians of the Galaxy received the transmission about Enchantress's escape.

"Hey, that's my home planet!" said Star-Lord. "Let's go help, and maybe pick up a hot dog while we're there."

"Why do we need a dog of any temperature?" asked Drax, as Gamora rolled her eyes.

Back on Earth, Spider-Man swung towards a bright light coming from Central Park.

"Whoa! It's too early for holiday lights," he said to himself. "Better check it out."

Spider-Man arrived in the park to find Enchantress reciting a spell, protected by an energy shield around her. Thor hovered above and did not look happy.

"We can do this the easy way or the hard way," said Thor.

Just then, the Guardians' ship landed nearby. "It's over, Enchantress," declared Thor. "You must surrender."

"You need to fight magic with magic," a voice called out. Everyone turned to see Doctor Strange, who was working up his own sorcery. "Let's see how the sorceress fares when she gets a taste of her own medicine." He began to summon a portal.

"No!" cried Enchantress. "The spell cannot be interrupted, or else…"

Just as the portal descended upon her, Enchantress's energy shield splintered into thousands of fragments of blinding light. For a moment, the whole world seemed to disappear.

"You're too late," said Enchantress. "My time spell will make me stronger than all of you."

"Wait!" Drax called into the void. "Or else what?"

Seconds later, Drax, Doctor Strange and Spider-Man found themselves in a strange field.

"Where are we?" asked Spider-Man.

Suddenly, an earth-shattering roar pierced the air.

"And what is that horrible noise?" asked Drax.

"Run!" cried Doctor Strange, as a herd of velociraptors barrelled down on them.

"Dinosaurs?" asked Spider-Man. "You have got to be kidding me!"

Doctor Strange used

his magic to levitate Drax and Spider-Man out of the velociraptors' paths. But it soon became clear the dinosaurs hadn't been running towards the Super Heroes…

… instead, they had been running away from something else.

A giant T-rex, to be exact.

"Uh-oh," said Spider-Man.

"Help me!" called a voice.

"Looks like we aren't the only ones who ended up here," said Spider-Man looking down.

Below them, trapped under a fallen tree, was the Enchantress.

"Quick," said Doctor Strange, setting Drax and Spidey back on the ground. "You two distract the T-rex. I'll handle her."

A pterodactyl flew by, giving Spider-Man an idea. He shot a web towards the pterodactyl, creating a lasso.

"Grab on!" he called to Drax, and the two heroes were lifted off the ground, swinging side to side. The T-rex below them was mesmerised as its eyes tracked their movements.

Once Doctor Strange freed the Enchantress from the tree, she turned to him, furious.

"I was trying to find a powerful magical stone, but your interference caused my time-travel spell to backfire. We've all been sent back in time!"

"Then we will need it to backfire again to get us back to our own time. And quickly," said Doctor Strange.

Enchantress summoned her powers and a beam of light began to grow around them. Just as the T-rex was about to stamp on them, the group disappeared with a poof!

"Gotcha!" cried Thor. The Enchantress fell right next to him as they all arrived back in the present. "You're coming to Asgard with me."

"Foiled again," said the Enchantress, sighing.

Thor peered at the group of heroes. "What happened?"

"We'll tell you all about it when we have the time," joked Spider-Man. "Get it?"

"I get it," said Drax, "it just wasn't very funny."

The Amazing Incredible Spider-Hulk

Spider-Man and the Avengers were having dinner. As the heroes ate, Iron Man challenged Hulk to an arm-wrestling contest.

"Too easy," said Hulk, as Iron Man struggled.

Spider-Man was a little jealous of his green pal. *I'm strong, but I'm not Hulk strong,* he thought. *If I could do everything the Hulk can do, I'd be the perfect Super Hero!*

Outside the restaurant, Spider-Man watched as the Hulk tried to sign a child's autograph book and crushed the pencil.

"Hey, big guy, why the frown?" asked Spidey.

Spider-Man was surprised to hear that the Hulk sometimes wanted to be, as he put it, "More puny, like Bug-Man."

"Isn't that something," began Spider-Man. "I was just thinking that I'd rather be more like you!"

At S.H.I.E.L.D. headquarters, everyone saw Nick Fury standing next to a high-tech device capped by an enormous purple gemstone. Fury explained that they were there to witness a demonstration of a machine that would allow two Super Heroes to temporarily swap abilities. This way, they could catch super villains off guard.

Spidey and the Hulk couldn't believe what they were hearing. It would be like switching places!

When Fury asked for volunteers, two hands immediately went up: a big green one and a smaller red one.

Spider-Man and the Hulk stood side by side over a big red X on the floor. Fury activated the device. The machine started to hum, and the purple gemstone glowed. It shot out a beam, covering both the Hulk and Spider-Man.

But the machine overheated, causing an explosion that shook the room! When the smoke cleared, everyone stared at the figure standing on the red X. It wasn't Spidey. It wasn't the Hulk. It looked like both of them… combined! Two heroes had merged into one hybrid creature – the Spider-Hulk!

Peering at Iron Man's armour, Spider-Hulk studied his reflection in its gleaming surface. The face that stared back was familiar, and yet… unfamiliar. Confused and frustrated, Spider-Hulk couldn't control his feelings. "Bug-Hulk SMASH!" he cried, pounding his fists into the floor.

Captain America tried to calm down the heroic hybrid. "At ease, soldier!" cried Cap, over the noise. But before he could continue, Spider-Hulk grabbed Cap's shield and flung it into the wall. Then, the frightened Spider-Hulk turned and crashed through the glass window. The Avengers raced after him.

Spider-Hulk didn't realise his pursuers were his friends, the Avengers.

"Bug-Hulk's bug-sense tingling," he muttered. He couldn't think clearly. It felt as though there were two separate voices in his head!

He just wanted to get away from the people trying to capture him.

Spider-Hulk used his webbing to outrun the Avengers, but when he twisted awkwardly, the web-line snapped and they fell onto the pavement below!

This gave Black Widow an idea. The Avengers would draw Spider-Hulk back to S.H.I.E.L.D. headquarters using the one thing both Spider-Man and the Hulk loved: food! When Thor and Black Widow found Spider-Hulk, he was ransacking every hot dog cart in the city. Thor stood in his path and tried to lure Spider-Hulk away with a delicious chocolate cake from the bakery.

With Spider-Hulk momentarily weakened, Hawkeye quickly came up with a plan. He had sometimes calmed the Hulk down with a nursery rhyme, so he sat down and began reading to Spider-Hulk. But the plan worked too well. The hybrid hero thought it was bedtime, and ran off to look for a midnight snack!

But before Thor could lead the way back to headquarters, Spider-Hulk swallowed the entire cake. The new Super Hero also had a super appetite!

Iron Man knew Spider-Man was really Peter Parker, a teenager who couldn't resist his Aunt May's famous wheatcakes. So the armoured Avenger instructed his personal chef to make enough wheatcakes to feed a small country. In other words, enough wheatcakes to feed a Spider-Hulk.

Iron Man zoomed around the city, leaving a trail of wheatcakes for his fused friend to follow. It worked! Spider-Hulk gobbled each tasty treat, leading him closer and closer to the device that caused all the chaos in the first place.

Spider-Hulk was so busy wolfing down wheatcakes that he didn't notice he was sitting on the big red X. He swallowed the last piece of wheatcake and said, "Spider-Hulk wants maple—"

But before he could finish his sentence, Nick Fury pressed the reverse button.

Once again the purple gemstone glowed and Spider-Hulk was shot with an energy beam.

When the light faded, two separate heroes stepped forth: Spider-Man and the Hulk!

"I really learned something today," Spider-Man told the Hulk. "I used to think I wanted to be more like you. But being Spider-Hulk just… didn't feel like me. And I like being me."

The green Goliath nodded. "Hulk learned something, too," he began. "Hulk learned that Bug-Man's puny costume is bad fit on Hulk-size body!" the two friends laughed. Then they patted their bellies and turned to the other Avengers.

"Okay," said Spider-Man, with a wink, "who's up for some dessert?"

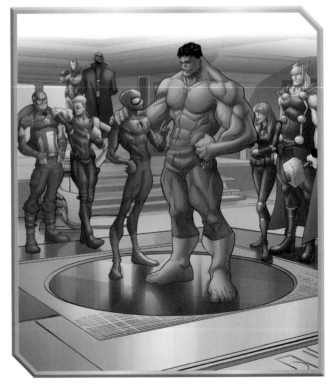

It was a good day to be Spider-Man. Earlier that morning, he had captured both Doctor Octopus and Sandman. Now, as the sun set, Spider-Man arrived at Avengers Tower. Nick Fury was there to greet him.

"Thanks for volunteering to keep an eye on the place while the Avengers are away," said Nick Fury.

Spider-Man replied, with a firm handshake, "Not only will I keep one eye on the place, I'll keep two!"

Spider-Man hoped that if he did this favour for the Avengers, they might let him join their team someday. Before Nick Fury left, he gave Spider-Man one important instruction: watch the security monitors.

"Don't worry, I've got this," said Spider-Man, confidently.

But watching the monitors was dull. So Spider-Man decided to do some exploring. His first stop was Tony Stark's lab. Inside, Spidey found a scroll that looked like a pirate's treasure map. But the scroll was covered in strange symbols. A note below the scroll read 'HANDS OFF!'

Spidey knew he shouldn't touch the map. The last time he fiddled around with mysterious artefacts in Tony's lab, he was sent back in time to the Old West. But his curiosity got the better of him! He held the map up to the light and saw glistening circuitry and bizarre icons woven throughout the parchment.

Without thinking, Spider-Man tapped one of the icons. An enormous portal opened up – and sucked the web-slinger right into it.

"Whoaaa! Not again!" cried Spidey, as he plunged deeper down the portal.

Dazed, Spidey realised he was being tied up by a huge, hairy man. The man grabbed the wall-crawler, yanking him forwards.

"'Tis a masked scurvy dog who appeared out o' nowhere, sir!" the man growled. A massive buccaneer with a braided beard turned to look at Spider-Man. It was Blackbeard the pirate!

"Oh, hello, Blackbeard, the most notorious pirate who ever lived," quipped Spider-Man. "I would love to stay and chat, but I better get going." Spider-Man attempted to flee, but the legendary pirate was not going to let Spider-Man go so easily.

Blackbeard eyed the map in Spidey's pocket. Thinking it was a treasure map, the pirate king snatched it. Then he shoved Spider-Man onto a wooden plank that jutted out over the waves. The web-slinger bumped into a man with a hook for a hand, who was already standing at the edge of the plank.

"I guess we're plankmates," Spidey joked to the man, who spun around to face him. It was Nick Fury!

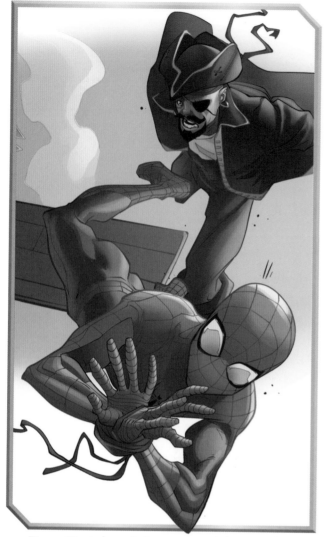

But before they could chat any further, Blackbeard knocked Fury and Spidey overboard!

Thinking quickly, Spidey used his super-strength to break through his bonds. Then he shot his webs and swung over the water, catching Fury in midair. Both of them were now safely on deck… or so they thought.

Spider-Man was untying Fury's ropes when Blackbeard's crew charged at them.

"Don't worry, I've got this," smirked Spidey, swiping Fury's hat. "Oh, and may I? I love a good costume!"

But Spider-Man quickly realised that this wasn't actually Nick Fury. Nick had once told Spider-Man a story about his ancestor.

"You're 'One-Eyed' Fury!" cried Spider-Man. "You're that English spy. Man, I thought Nick was pulling my leg."

"Will you keep your voice down, sir!" said One-Eyed Fury, in a loud whisper. "I'm undercover."

"How's that working out for you so far?" asked Spidey.

Spider-Man covered the attacking pirates with a net of webbing. Then he tossed the webbed swashbucklers at the remaining pirates, making them scatter like billiard balls.

"Eight ball in the corner pirate!"

Suddenly, Blackbeard snapped his fingers and two ferocious female buccaneers appeared.

"Ahoy, scallywags! May I introduce ye to me buckos Sandy Dunes 'n' Doctor Squidlegs," boomed Blackbeard. "Ladies, attack!"

Spidey turned to One-Eyed Fury. "I can't understand a word this guy says."

Doctor Squidlegs's mechanical tentacles hissed and clicked as they came down all around Spider-Man and One-Eyed Fury, while Sandy Dunes whipped up a huge sandstorm.

But Spider-Man and One-Eyed Fury were ready!

One-Eyed Fury. "Watch this!" The spy pressed a button on his sleeve and his hook hand transformed into a water cannon. A jet of water sprayed out of the cannon, melting Sandy Dunes!

Suddenly, the deck began to shake. Blackbeard had used the map to open a portal! Thinking quickly, One-Eyed Fury used his water cannon to pummel the famous pirate and his comrades, knocking them out cold.

"Not bad for a guy with one eye… and one hand," said Spider-Man, as he grabbed the map and jumped through the portal.

The two heroes worked together as a team to take on the villains.

"Follow my lead, Fury!" cried Spider-Man, as he covered Doctor Squidlegs in webs.

"Is that all you got?" asked

"Thank you, sir!" called out One-Eyed Fury, as he took control of the ship. "I hope we meet again!"

As Spider-Man entered the portal, he could've sworn he saw something else fly through the portal with him.

The portal dropped Spider-Man back in the present day.

That was way more fun than watching monitors, thought Spider-Man. *Wait, the monitors!*

Spidey rushed back to make sure nothing bad had happened while he was gone. Everything looked quiet enough, except for a flash of movement on one screen. It was Blackbeard's parrot, and Spider-Man had to catch the feathered felon before it wrecked all the furniture in Avengers Tower!

Ghost-Spider
Gwen Stacy

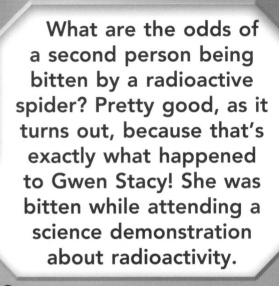

What are the odds of a second person being bitten by a radioactive spider? Pretty good, as it turns out, because that's exactly what happened to Gwen Stacy! She was bitten while attending a science demonstration about radioactivity.

- **Height: 5' 5"**
- **Occupation: Student**
- **Superhuman strength**
- **Superhuman agility**
- **Superhuman endurance**
- **Sticking to and climbing walls and other surfaces**
- **Mechanical web-shooters, allowing her to fire and swing from sticky webs**
- **'Spider-sense' that warns of incoming danger**
- **Can lift approx. ten tons**

Spider-Man
Miles Morales

Guess what! Peter Parker and Gwen Stacy aren't the only spiders in town! Meet Miles Morales, a high school student and friend of Peter Parker and Gwen Stacy. Miles was bitten by – you guessed it – a spider! This one was genetically modified instead of radioactive.

- Height: 5' 7"
- Occupation: Student
- Superhuman strength
- Superhuman agility
- Superhuman endurance
- Sticking to and climbing walls and other surfaces
- Web-shooters
- Can camouflage himself and his clothing, becoming nearly invisible
- Discharges powerful electrical venom strikes
- 'Spider-sense' that warns of incoming danger

The New Spider-Man in Town

Miles Morales was a student at Midtown High School in New York City. He was happy and had a thirst for knowledge, especially science. He was a young boy just like any other, working hard and doing the right thing, but something soon happened that changed his life for good...

When in chemistry class, Miles noticed that his good friend, Peter Parker, kept sneaking out of school. Miles grew suspicious, wondering if something was wrong with Peter.

So one day, Miles followed Peter and watched as he sneaked a mask from his bag. But it wasn't just any mask that Peter was sneaking – it was Spider-Man's mask!

Miles couldn't believe it. When Peter was leaving school that afternoon, Miles called to Peter, "Hey, Peter, where are you headed?"

Peter awkwardly smiled back and said, "Uh, I've got an assignment for the *Daily Bugle*... uh... yeah... I've... I've got to go!"

Miles followed Peter to a lab, but lost track of him. Miles didn't notice a genetically altered spider slowly spinning a web and dropping down towards him.

Instead of getting ill from the bite, Miles soon discovered that it gave him spider powers. "I've got to figure out what this means! What should I do?"

He ran home fast.

"Think! Think! Think," Miles told himself. "If Peter really is Spider-Man, then what did he do?" Miles searched for articles about the webbed wonder. "Okay, so you get powers. Check. Then what? You make a costume and go stop bad guys. That seems obvious!"

With that, Miles created his own Spider-Man costume and leapt into the city.

"YEE-OW!"

The spider bit Miles right on the hand! Miles knocked it off. He knew instantly that this was no ordinary spider bite.

"I can run on walls!" cried Miles, as he scaled the side of a building. He was enjoying discovering his powers, and climbing walls wasn't the only one! Miles soon discovered he had an amazing spider-sense that warned him of danger.

"What the heck?" Miles couldn't ignore the ringing in his brain. That's when he noticed the burglars running behind him. In that instant, what started off as fun became very scary.

Miles had a really big decision to make. Should he run from the danger and stay safe, or should he use his new powers to try to stop the villains?

Miles realised that if he was going to call himself Spider-Man, he was going to have to act like Spider-Man, too.

Much to his surprise, Peter Parker, as the original Spider-Man, was already on the case! One of the criminals was getting away, but Miles joined in. "Hold on helmet head," he announced. "The only place you're racing off to is prison!"

Miles had powers to match Peter's and was easily able to contain the thief.

It wasn't until the action was over that Miles realised just how much danger he was really in. He climbed to the top of a building and wanted to fade away – which is exactly what he did.

This was a brand-new power, one that even Peter didn't have! He camouflaged himself into his surroundings.

Peter swung up to where Miles had been. "Miles, is that you?" Peter called out. "I recognised your voice. Believe it or not, I know what you're thinking. I went through the same thing when I first got my powers."

Miles was stunned. "You did?"

"Sure, I did," said Peter. "My Uncle Ben used to tell me that with great power, there must also come great responsibility."

Peter tossed Miles something from his costume. "Here, you can have these extra web-shooters for now," said Peter.

"Whoa! Cool!" said Miles, while testing out the web-shooters.

Miles looked at Peter, trying to figure out what he should do.

"Maybe I can follow you around for a few days," he said. "You know, see how it goes?"

"I think that's a good idea, but you can't go around calling yourself Spider-Man, Miles. That name's taken."

"Oh, I'm definitely Spider-Man," said Miles, smiling again. The two swung off together to patrol their neighbourhood.

And that's when Miles knew he was born for this!

The battle roared while Peter kept poking fun at the rampaging villains. Miles was terrified. "How do you keep joking in the middle of a fight?" he asked Peter. "Aren't you scared?"

That's when Rhino grabbed Peter by the neck. Peter couldn't let out another word, funny or otherwise.

Miles turned and let loose his newest and last power – another power that Peter didn't have at all. Miles would later call it his venom strike. It put Rhino down for the count and Peter was safe.

It wasn't long before Peter had them in quite a pickle, surrounded by some of the nastiest villains in New York City!

Miles and Peter wrapped the baddies up in enough webbing to stop their dastardly scheme.

Peter said, "Come on, if you're not going to change your name, you've got to learn how to crack jokes – it's part of the job."

Miles scratched his head, thinking while looking down at the webbed-up villains. Then he said, "Looks like you've got yourselves into a sticky situation, uh, evil-doers."

Peter sighed. "Wow. Somebody call the doctor, you have no funny bone."

Peter Parker was at the cinema with his best friends, Miles Morales and Gwen Stacy. Suddenly, the whole room went pitch black!

"Oh, man," groaned Miles. "They were just about to catch the bad guys."

A member of staff addressed the complaining crowd. "Sorry, folks," he said. "We're having a power outage. Must be due to the lightning storm outside."

Lightning storm? The three friends exchanged worried looks.

"Let's check it out," said Gwen.

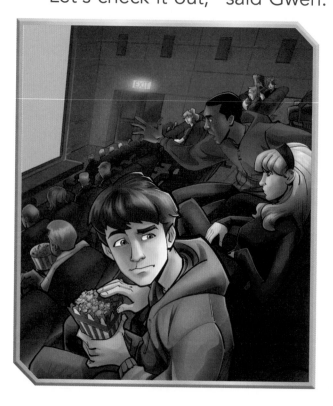

Outside in Times Square, the scene was frantic – someone had taken over all the city's power!

"My spider-sense is tingling," murmured Gwen, warily.

"Mine, too," said Miles, cautiously.

"That makes three of us," confirmed Peter. "One day I'd like my spider-sense to point me to the nearest hot dog stand."

The three heroes quickly ducked into an alley to change into their spider-costumes.

"It looks like Electro is up to his old tricks," said Peter. "He wants to use the city's electricity to strengthen his powers."

"We need to stop him before this becomes dangerous," said Gwen Stacy.

Suddenly, there was a loud CRASH as a lorry collided with a car!

Miles swung off on his own to track Electro. *I'll show them,* thought Miles. *My plan will work, and then I'll be the hero. ZZZZZZZZ!*

Miles heard a loud buzzing and followed it down to the subway tunnels, only to find Electro! He was absorbing the energy from the subway tracks.

Miles accidentally kicked a stray can of fizzy pop, attracting Electro's attention.

"What's this?" said Electro, smirking. "Not another Spider-Man?"

Thinking quickly, Miles fired a venom blast at the super villain... but he missed.

"You must still be in training," said Electro, laughing madly.

Angered, Miles tried again, this time with his web-shooters, but Electro shot back with a lightning bolt that knocked him out cold.

"You better come with me, Mini-Spider," said Electro, as he tossed Miles over his shoulder and ran off down the subway tunnel.

Suddenly, a familiar voice came from behind the super villain. "Electro, why so blue?"

THWIP!

It was Ghost-Spider! She fired her web-shooters, trying to capture Electro.

ZAP!

Electro blasted lightning bolts and knocked a stunned Ghost-Spider backwards.

Spider-Man leapt up onto the ceiling and tried to wrap a web around the limp Miles, so as to pull the hero towards him.

Meanwhile, at the city's energy-control centre, Electro had taken Miles and the facility-workers prisoner. The villain stood in front of a giant control panel.

"Once I hack into the system, I will be unstoppable," cried Electro.

WHOOOOSH!

Just then, a train came thundering through the tunnel.

Spider-Man grabbed Ghost-Spider just in time. They clung to the wall as the train roared past. Once it was clear, they hopped down and looked around.

Electro and Miles were gone. Spider-Man and Ghost-Spider searched New York City, hoping to track down their friend, Miles, and their not-so-friendly enemy, Electro.

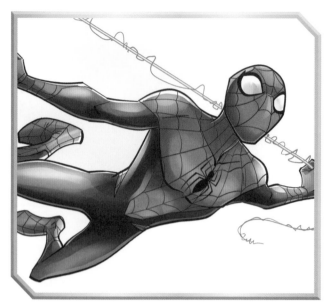

While Electro was distracted, Ghost-Spider crept in quietly and freed Miles. Before Electro knew what hit him, she swooped in and fired a pair of webs that pinned Electro against the wall.

But Electro quickly broke free from the webbing.

"MWAAHHHHHH!" he roared, electricity coursing through him.

He fired a supercharged lightning bolt that sent all three wall-crawlers ducking for cover.

"Miles," whispered Ghost-Spider, "your venom blast. It's the only way."

"I think you've caused enough mischief for today," said Spider-Man, as he suddenly burst into the control room.

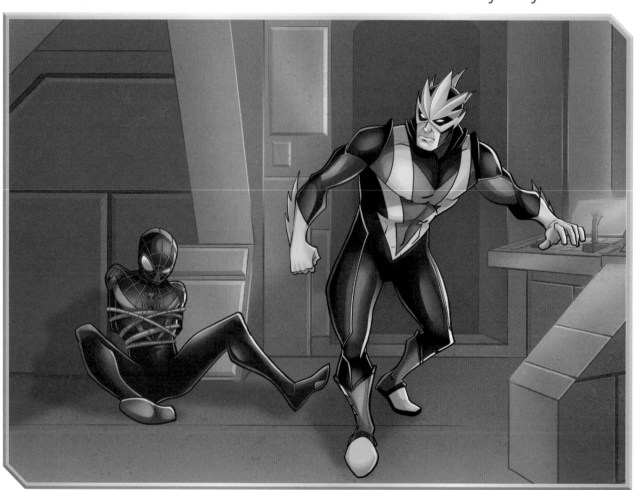

Miles was hesitant. What if he missed Electro again?

"Don't worry," Spider-Man encouraged Miles. "We'll do this together."

With the help of his pals, Miles summoned his courage and fired his venom blast at Electro, shocking the super villain while he was fully-charged.

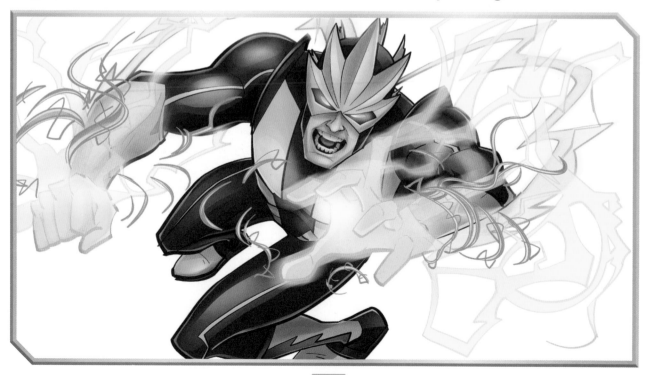

Immediately, Electro began to short-circuit.

With Electro beaten, the trio changed and headed back to the cinema.

"Thanks for having my back," Miles told his friends.

"You're an important part of this team," said Gwen, smiling.

"Wow, my spider-sense is tingling," said Peter.

"Mine isn't—" began Miles, until he nearly bumped into hot dog stand. All three of them laughed, and Miles said, "Movies, hot dogs and catching bad guys. This is definitely the team for me!"

Young Miles Morales and his friend Ganke were on a school trip when they were caught by surprise. "Ganke, watch out!" Miles shouted to his best friend.

A flood of wild animals came stampeding towards them right in the heart of the Central Park Zoo!

Miles knew he had to help, but he couldn't put on his spider-suit. Ganke was the only non-Super Hero who knew about his powers. Putting on his suit would reveal Miles's secret identity to everyone!

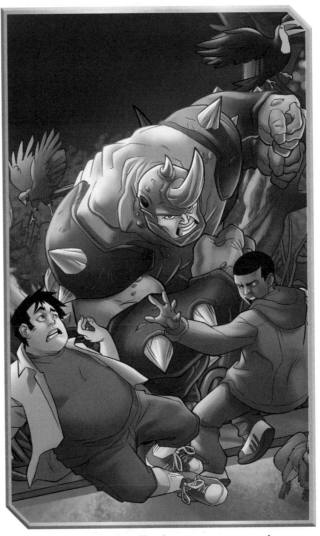

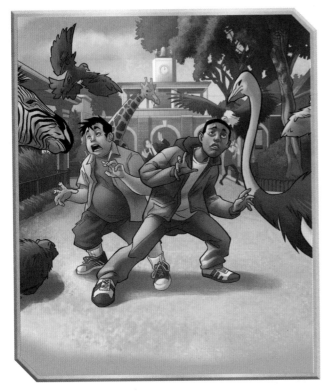

"How did all these animals escape?" asked Ganke.

As if the universe was answering his question, Rhino charged out of the woods and came barrelling down on Miles and Ganke.

"Jump, dude!" Ganke shouted at Miles. "He's going to run you over!"

Luckily for Miles, the original Spider-Man snagged Rhino's horn just in time to save Miles from revealing his secret, and from a LOT of bruises.

"Yeehaw! You're worse than a bucking bronco, Rhino!" shouted Spider-Man.

When Miles realised that THE Spider-Man was there to help, he was thrilled.

Rhino jerked his head away, yanking Spidey off his back.

WHAM!

Spidey slammed down into the ground.

"Ha!" bellowed Rhino. "Try and keep up, Spider-Man. My new animal friends and I are pretty wild."

As Peter lay on his back, Miles rushed over to see if he was okay. "Hey, Pe— uh, I mean, Spider-Man," said Miles.

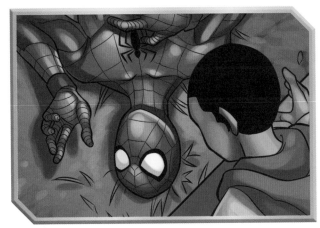

Peter was still a little woozy from hitting the ground.

"Miles! Great to see you, buddy—"

But before Peter could finish, he felt Rhino's hand grab his ankle.

Rhino flung Spidey through the air. As Peter whizzed by, he asked Miles, "How are your grades holding uuuup?"

Miles stood face-to-face with Rhino, but he didn't budge. Not one inch.

"You've got nerve kid," snorted Rhino. "You're lucky I got the web-head to finish, otherwise I'd teach you a lesson!"

Rhino stormed off to find Peter Parker. He didn't realise that Miles was also a Spider-Man.

Miles looked left and right. All of his classmates, even Ganke, were gone! He remembered what Peter once told him: "With great power comes great responsibility."

Without a second thought, Miles slipped on his mask and pulled on his suit.

Where Miles once stood, now bounced the one and only (well, one of only two) Spider-Man! Miles's kick to Rhino's head was enough to give Peter a chance to get loose from the super villain's grip!

"Thanks for the assist, Spider-Man," said Peter.

"How cute, the Spider-Men have come to meet their doom," snarled Rhino.

As Peter dodged Rhino's attacks, he called to Miles, "I need you to wrangle the zoo animals before they cause any more damage!"

Miles was hurt. "You don't want my help battling Rhino?"

Before Peter could respond, Rhino poked his horn right into Peter's behind!

Why does Peter not want my help? thought Miles. *Maybe I'm not cut out for this whole Super Hero thing after all.*

But just when Miles began to doubt himself, he remembered there was a job to do. It was his responsibility to wrangle the animals, and if that's what Peter needed, then that's exactly what he was going to do!

With great care, Miles wrestled a crocodile, webbing its mouth so it couldn't bite anyone.

Using his wall-crawling ability, Miles climbed a tree to help a cute red panda to safety.

Then, Miles contained a lion by electrifying the air using his venom strike. Eventually, Miles had helped all the animals find their habitats.

As Miles stood in front of the contained animals, he began to wonder where Peter and Rhino were.

"Ow. Ow. OW!" Suddenly, Peter came bouncing across the pavement and slammed to a stop next to Miles.

"Rough landing," joked Peter. "Man, where's another Spider-Man when you need him?"

"Seriously, dude?" asked Miles.

Even though Miles was still learning his powers, Peter knew he was ready. "What do you say, Miles – you want to see if Rhino can beat the Spider-Men?"

Miles smiled. "I thought you'd never ask!"

Together, the Spider-Men made the ultimate team.

"Have a nice trip!" said Peter, as he webbed up Rhino's feet.

"Man, your ugly mug is shocking!" said Miles, as he used his venom strike to give Rhino an unexpected jolt.

"Oooh, nice one!" cheered Peter.

Rhino slammed into the pavement, knocking himself out cold. "Do you want to make the final wisecrack?" asked Peter.

Miles smiled. "How's this? 'Spider-Men: we put the NO in Rhino'."

Peter burst into laughter and let out a theatrical sob. "My little baby is all grown up!"

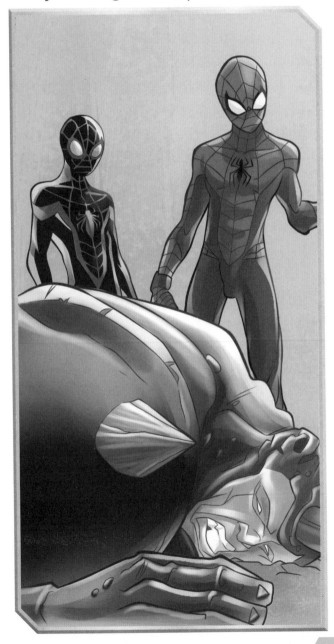

After taking care of Rhino, the Spider-Men settled down for a well-deserved lunch break. "Remember when I told you that true heroes give back to their community?" asked Peter.

Miles nodded as he took a loud sip of his drink.

"Well, giving the Central Park Zoo a dude dressed as a Rhino wasn't exactly what I had in mind."

Miles grinned. "Still... he definitely fits in."

Shock & Awe

Peter Parker sat down on a rooftop ledge next to his friend and Super Hero partner, Gwen Stacy. He'd had a long night fighting baddies. Peter let out a long sigh.

"Okay," said Gwen, also known as Ghost-Spider. "Spill it. What's wrong?"

"Huh?" said Peter, confused. "Oh, I'm sorry. I'm just tired. I haven't slept." He rubbed his forehead. "There've been these robberies, and I can't figure out who's doing them."

"Well, talk to me," said Gwen. "Maybe you just need a fresh set of eyes… I mean ears."

"Every night, a couple of technology targets are hit," began Peter. "Computer shops, tech start-ups, places like that."

"And at every location," he continued, "the security systems are shorted out. They're completely fried. I figured it was Electro, but I checked, he's behind bars."

Peter looked defeated. "So if it's not Electro, then who could it be?" he wondered aloud.

"That's odd! There've been a string of robberies in my neighbourhood, too," said Gwen. "Homes, a grocery… even a toy shop. But there's no sign of forced entry at any of them. I don't even know how the thief is getting in. When I tried to find out, the only thing I could find was some wet footprints. All the crime scenes had them."

"I think I know who's robbing the shops in your neighbourhood," said Peter.

"I think we've got that in common," said Gwen, triumphantly. "Because I know who's robbing those electronics shops."

The friends grinned.

Gwen and Peter put their heads together, working out detail after detail, idea after idea. They found that in using one another's strengths, they made a pretty good team. All they had to do was build the trap.

Or in their case, a web.

The first thing they needed to do was find a target that would attract both criminals.

An empty shopfront in Gwen's neighbourhood fit the bill perfectly.

With a freshly printed banner and a foggy front window, they disguised the shopfront as an up-and-coming electronics shop. Peter passed out flyers and Gwen posted on all the top social media sites and tech blogs.

Their web had been spun.

Now it was just a matter of waiting for the sun to go down.

With everything in place, Spider-Man and Ghost-Spider perched on the rooftop of their fake shop. They waited in silence, hoping to spot anything unusual.

"Yawn…"

Spider-Man was having trouble keeping his eyes open. But suddenly his spider-sense jolted him wide-awake.

He scanned the street below and saw a thin stream of water making its way towards the building. It was as if the water was alive.

The water slid underneath the shop's metal shutter. It moved a few feet into the dark room, then lifted itself up into the air. Slowly but surely, it took the shape of a person.

Electricity shot out of the figure's hands and into the automatic lock on the back door.

Ghost-Spider smiled beneath her mask. "I knew it," she whispered.

Her gaze met Spider-Man's and, with a nod, they took action.

Inside the shop, the shadowy figure's hands began to glow. Spider-Man's suspicions had been correct: Electro was behind the group of recent tech robberies.

There stood the villain Spider-Man suspected had been ransacking Ghost-Spider's neighbourhood: Hydro-Man!

Meanwhile, Ghost-Spider spotted a shadowy figure approaching the back of the building. She ducked down low, keeping her gaze on the mysterious stranger.

KKKZZZAAAPPP!

Just not the Electro he'd thought.

There in the darkness was the newest electrically-powered villain to plague New York City: Francine Frye.

The first thing Electro noticed was that this 'shop' wasn't much of a shop at all. The second thing she noticed was a dark figure standing at the opposite end of the large room.

It's a trap, thought Electro. She immediately disengaged her electric charge. Now more than ever, she would need to stick to the shadows.

Across the shop, Hydro-Man saw a spark of light out of the corner of his eye. He strained to see in the darkness. He could only make out a dark shadow standing by the open back door. Someone was waiting for him!

Hydro-Man clenched his fists. He was not one to give up without a fight.

The two villains bided their time. Then, at nearly the exact same moment, Hydro-Man lashed out with a blast of water while Electro shot a giant bolt of electricity from her hands!

FFFZZZAAACRRRACCKKK!

Lightning met water in a tremendous explosion!

Sparks, smoke and steam filled the room. Ghost-Spider took advantage of the chaos and leapt forward towards Electro, keeping her from causing further damage and mayhem.

Hydro-Man staggered backwards. He had received such a shock to his system, he couldn't even think about turning into water at the moment. It was all he could do to try to keep his balance. Just then, Spider-Man leapt from the shadows.

"So this is what happens when you don't pay your water bill," he joked as he shot a web towards his opponent.

Hydro-Man hit the floor with a thud. He was down for the count.

Later, back on the rooftop, the heroes watched as S.H.I.E.L.D. agents carted away the two villains.

"What did I tell you?" said Gwen, happily. "A fresh perspective was all either of us needed. Now you can go home and finally get some rest!"

But Peter didn't answer. He had fallen asleep ten minutes ago.

Venom
Eddie Brock

Venom is one weird dude! Part-man and part-alien creature, Venom really doesn't like Spider-Man and his friends. He also has most of the same powers as Spider-Man. Venom can climb walls, and he is super-strong. Oh, and let's not forget about the scary teeth!

- Height: Variable

- Occupation: Troublemaker

- Symbiotic being who has bonded itself to a human host

- Amorphous costume-like entity who can take a variety of shapes and camouflage itself

- Grants its host superhuman strength, agility and durability

- Extrudes tendrils and a long tongue

- Can create and project a web-like fluid from its own substance

- Member of the Sinister Six

A Sticky Situation

Gwen was putting the finishing touches to a sound cannon she'd been working on.

But it was soon time to start training.

"Let's go through a couple of simple training exercises," said Spider-Man a few minutes later, once they'd got to the roof. "Make sure to pay attention. You've got to work hard if you want to be a Super Hero."

One sunny day, Spider-Man was helping an old lady. She thought there was a smelly goo monster in the sewers.

"That's just our wonderfully stinky city," said Spider-Man, reassuringly.

He then swung away to meet up with Miles and Gwen for a training session.

After changing out of his suit, Peter joined Gwen and Miles at the school science lab.

To begin, Miles tried out his improved bio-electric venom blasts. But Spider-Man was able to dodge every single one.

"Your venom blasts are too wild and uncontrolled," said Spider-Man, as he leapt all over Miles. "You're not focusing on your target."

On the street below, long black tendrils suddenly appeared out of the sewers and began throwing unsuspecting citizens into the air. The heroes used their webbing to safely catch them all.

A big, black creature emerged from the spiralling tendrils.

"Venom," said Spider-Man.

Ghost-Spider knew the name well. "The alien that bonded itself to a human host named Eddie Brock!" she exclaimed.

"You don't really want to hurt people, Eddie!" called out Spider-Man.

Gwen, also known as Ghost-Spider, rolled her eyes. "Know-it-all."

Suddenly, Ghost-Spider's spider-sense began tingling.

"Eddie can't hear you, Sssssspider-Man," the villain hissed. "There'sssss only Venom now."

The heroes had no option but to fight the gooey villain.

Spider-Man flung himself away from Venom's creeping tendrils. "Ghost-Spider, you make sure the civilians are safe," he ordered. "Miles, it might be time to put those improved bio-electric blasts to work."

THWIP!

He shot his sticky webbing in Venom's face. It looked like Spider-Man had saved the day, when…

SMACK!

Venom ripped the webbing off his face and knocked Spider-Man out cold.

Venom swung his tendrils in all directions, smashing everything in sight.

Miles aimed his blasts at the super villain, as Ghost-Spider caught a piece of falling rubble.

"And now your friendly neighbourhood web-head swings in for the grand finale," said Spider-Man.

Miles fired off a round of venom blasts at a large electronic screen, causing a shower of sparks to rain down on Venom.

"Be right back!" called Ghost-Spider.

She quickly returned with her sound cannon. "Plug your ears," she said. "I'm about to turn things up."

Ghost-Spider pulled Spidey to safety. "I know how to take him down for good," she said to Miles. But I'll need you to keep him distracted for a couple of minutes."

Ghost-Spider unleashed the full power of the sound cannon on Venom. He struggled to maintain his monstrous form as the sound waves hit him.

"Ssssstop!" he screeched.

"Keep going!" exclaimed Miles.

Soon, Venom's body reverted to a puddle of goo, revealing Eddie Brock's human form underneath.

As Eddie was taken away by the police, Spider-Man woke up. Even in his confused state, he felt bad that he hadn't thought his friends were ready to help him fight crime.

"I was wrong earlier when I said all you've got to do is work hard," said Spider-Man. "A real hero also needs to work smart, like both of you did, especially if they're going to wear a spider on their chest." He paused. "I'm glad we're a team."

Suddenly, the old lady from earlier appeared. "I told you it was a goo monster!" she cried.

Spider-Man cringed. "Sorry, ma'am. I'll make sure to double-check next time."

With that, the three heroes swung away.

Kraven the Hunter
Sergei Kravinoff

Kraven is the world's most famous hunter, and often comes to New York City to try and capture the most dangerous and elusive prey of all, the wondrous wall-crawler! But Spidey always foils the hunter's evil schemes.

- Height: 6' 0"
- Occupation: Game hunter
- Seeks to defeat Spider-Man to prove he's the greatest hunter in the world
- Utilises hand-to-hand combat and expert knife-fighting
- After ingesting a mythical potion, he was given superhuman strength, speed, stamina and durability
- Master hunter and tracker
- Member of the Sinister Six

Kraven the Hunter loved to hunt wild animals. The only thing he loved more was the fame that came along with it. But one day, after Kraven had captured a pair of cheetahs, he didn't feel the same sense of accomplishment he normally felt after a successful hunt.

Kraven hungered for a new prey that would give him a real challenge. But where could he find such a foe?

A few days later, Peter Parker was sent by the *Daily Bugle* to photograph the annual Protection of Endangered Animals conference in Upper Manhattan. Giving the keynote speech was none other than T'Challa, ruler of the African nation of Wakanda.

Peter was excited for the chance to see T'Challa speak. The king was a compassionate ruler and a scientific genius.

Black Panther protected his nation and its animal kingdom from villains by using his superhuman strength, speed and agility. One of those villains was Kraven the Hunter.

Desperate for a new challenge, Kraven knew that this conference was the perfect place to find his next prey, Black Panther! The villain burst through a window in a spray of broken glass.

"T'Challa!" he bellowed loudly. "I request a meeting with the Black Panther."

T'Challa's eyes narrowed. "Black Panther will never bow to the likes of you!"

But T'Challa had a secret. He was also the Super Hero Black Panther!

"In order to protect the animals of Earth," the king began, "it is our duty to fight back against illegal hunters and poachers."

Kraven gave an evil smirk. "I assumed there would be some protest. That's why I brought some backup!"

Kraven let out a high-pitched whistle, and two cheetahs leapt down from the window above.

"No one here is allowed to leave until the Black Panther is mine!"

In the chaos, Peter Parker's spider-senses were tingling like crazy. He knew he had to act fast. This place was turning into a zoo!

Meanwhile, T'Challa's bodyguards, the Dora Milaje, attempted to move the Wakandan king to safety.

"Save your energy," T'Challa commanded. "It's time for Black Panther to strike."

"Spider-Man, no! You must be careful!" Black Panther tried to warn the web-slinger, but it was already too late.

"Whoa! Nice kitty!" exclaimed Spider-Man as the cheetah grabbed his web and lunged towards him.

Black Panther turned around to discover that he had been joined by Spider-Man!

"What are you doing here?" asked Black Panther.

"Nice to see you, too," replied Spider-Man, swinging into action.

Spider-Man fired a ball of web fluid at the nearest cheetah. "Stand back, I've beaten Kraven before. I can deal with these overgrown house cats."

Acting fast, Black Panther grabbed the cheetah before Spider-Man was harmed.

"Listen to me," he told Spidey. "My animal instincts tell me that these creatures are being held here against their will. They will only attack you if they are provoked."

Spidey wasn't out of danger yet! Kraven aimed a deadly spear at the web-slinger, but Spidey rolled out of the way just in time!

"I'll calm the cheetahs down while you get Kraven," said Black Panther to Spidey.

"On it!" said Spider-Man, as he swung towards the balcony.

Kraven had found a way to increase the aggression of the cheetahs, but luckily Black Panther had a special understanding of wildlife. He massaged the backs of the cheetahs' heads and safely pressed down on their pressure points to relax the animals' anger.

"That should calm you down," he said, petting them gently.

With the cheetahs under control, Spider-Man caught up with the villainous hunter.

"I did not come here for you, Spider-Man, but if I must capture you, too, so be it!" said Kraven.

He began to throw knives at the web-slinging hero, but Spidey's trusty spider-sense made it impossible for Kraven to land an attack.

"What's the matter, Kraven?" asked Spider-Man. "Can't catch a little spider?"

He continued, jokingly, "Maybe it would help if you took care of the smell first. P-U! Or do they not have showers in the jungle?"

Blinded with anger, Kraven was unable to focus on the fight with the two Super Heroes. Spider-Man quickly used his web-shooters to disarm Kraven,

giving Black Panther the perfect opening for an attack.

"Now you will pay for the crimes you have committed against the animal kingdom!" added Black Panther, before delivering the final blow to Kraven. The hunter was clearly no match for the strength and speed of the King of Wakanda.

Kraven was finally defeated.

"What's wrong? Don't like being held in captivity?" asked Spidey.

Black Panther addressed the crowd. "These majestic creatures are not the enemy," he told them. "They deserve respect and compassion. And thank you, Spider-Man, for helping me save them."

Spider-Man was caught off guard by the Black Panther's kind words. "Wow. Thanks, Black Panther. Now might not be a good time, but do you mind if we take a selfie?"

Mysterio
Quentin Beck

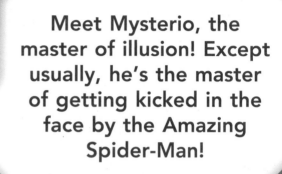

Meet Mysterio, the master of illusion! Except usually, he's the master of getting kicked in the face by the Amazing Spider-Man!

- Height: 5' 11"
- Occupation: Criminal mastermind
- Master of physical stunt work and mechanical and visual special effects
- Suit includes glass helmet with thirty minute air supply, holographic projectors, as well as gloves and boots that emit hallucinogenic gas that can render Spider-Man's spider-sense useless
- Skilled actor
- Trained in hypnotism and basic psychiatry
- Created his own version of Spider-Man's webbing
- Member of the Sinister Six

Mysterio's Revenge

Spider-Man shot a web across Fifth Avenue and swung past the Empire State Building. He was on his way towards the *Daily Bugle*. Peter Parker was late for work and the only thing that could get him there in time was his web-shooters.

"Great," Peter said to himself, as he fired another web. "If I'm late for work again, Mr Jameson is going to explode!"

Just then, an explosion of green and purple smoke erupted from the top floor of the *Daily Bugle* building!

"Yikes! I didn't think he'd literally explode!" said Spidey. "Better get in there to see if anyone needs help."

Landing on the side of the building, Spider-Man crawled up the wall and looked through the window into the smoky office. That's when he heard a booming voice and his spider-sense started to tingle.

"Now that I have your attention," the bizarre voice began, "you will all witness the total destruction of the *Daily Bugle*!"

Spider-Man recognised that voice – it was his enemy Mysterio, who was the master of illusion!

The menacing Mysterio was holding J. Jonah Jameson by the tie and addressing the terrified staff.

"No one can help you now, Jameson, not even Spider-Man!" the villain hissed.

"That's my cue!" said Spidey, as he launched himself at the villain. Spider-Man caught Mysterio by surprise and the two tumbled to the ground, locked in combat!

As the Super Hero and super villain continued to fight, Jameson crawled to the exit. He jiggled the doorknob frantically, but all the doors had been locked from the outside. They were trapped inside the building!

"It's the Amazing Spider-Man!" began Mysterio. "You're right on time... to meet your doom!"

Mysterio raised his arms and the newsroom filled with thick green smoke. Then the villain disappeared into the swirling fog right before everyone's astonished eyes!

"Meet my doom?" said Spider-Man. "What do you suppose he meant by that?"

Mysterio's voice echoed eerily across the room.

"Last time I saw you, J. Jonah Jameson, you promised that you could deliver Spider-Man," the villain cried. "Instead, I was defeated by Spider-Man... and now you will all pay the price!"

With that, Mysterio appeared through the smoke and lunged at Jameson.

Spider-Man knew he had to act fast! He fired a web and swung towards the villain. With unbelievable strength and speed, he kicked Mysterio in the chest and fired another web at Jameson, sticking him to the wall.

"Sorry to disappoint you, Mysterio, but I don't plan to meet my doom for at least another sixty or seventy years!" said Spidey.

Spider-Man stood above the trapped Mysterio and removed the villain's glass helmet. But Spidey was shocked at the person he saw beneath the mask: it was himself – Peter Parker!

"Parker!" yelled Jameson. "You're Mysterio?"

Only Spider-Man knew that the villain wasn't really Peter Parker.

This must've been the disguise Mysterio was going to use in order to escape, thought Spidey. But how was Spider-Man going to save everyone in the *Daily Bugle* and prove that Mysterio wasn't Peter? While all these thoughts ran through Spidey's mind, the villain leapt forward and attacked!

Ow, I hit hard! thought Spidey. As he tried to pick himself up off the floor, Mysterio delivered another hard blow. *I can't believe I'm beating myself up!*

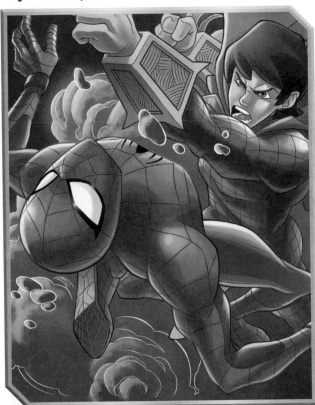

Spider-Man was dazed, but he rolled across the smoky room. With Mysterio distracted by his precious helmet, Spidey looked around the office and realised the only person who wasn't there was himself, the real Peter Parker. That's why Mysterio used him for his disguise! And that gave the wall-crawler an idea.

Spidey crawled along the wall, hidden by the smoke. He grabbed a hoodie off a desk, zipped it up to cover his suit and removed his mask. Now it looked like the real Peter Parker had shown up.

"Hey guys. Sorry I'm late."

Mysterio turned, enraged. "No! How did you get in?"

"Two Parkers?" said Jameson, confused. "Next there will be two Spider-Men!"

"Not if I have anything to say about it!" cried Mysterio.

The appearance of the real Peter Parker had worked. While everyone was distracted, Peter ducked beneath the smoke, put his mask back on and charged at Mysterio.

A few minutes later, the real Peter Parker entered the newsroom. J. Jonah Jameson, who was still stuck to the side of the wall, looked down at him. "Parker," he said, "you're late!"

Peter sighed. It was just another day at the office for Peter Parker... and your friendly neighbourhood Spider-Man!

Firing both web-shooters again and again, the Amazing Spider-Man captured Mysterio in a giant spiderweb for all to see.

Then, with a CRASH, the police finally broke into the newsroom, just as Spider-Man jumped out the nearest window.

"Here you go, boys," Spidey said to the cops as he swung away. "A gift-wrapped villain, courtesy of you-know-who!"

Chameleon
Dmitri Smerdyakov

Not only is Chameleon a spy, he is also a master of disguise. Chameleon realised he could use this to his advantage! Now he can make himself look like anyone else. He can even trick Super Heroes into thinking he is one of the good guys! Which makes him a pretty bad guy.

- Height: Unknown
- Occupation: Professional criminal
- Master of disguise
- Initially designed a costume that could mimic any clothing, including a holographic belt that could store the appearances of people he came into contact with to use whenever he needed
- Eventually used a serum that allowed him to change his appearance at will

The Widow's Sting

Spider-Man was casually swinging through the streets of New York City. It was the weekend, and crime-fighting had been kind of quiet, not that he was complaining. Sometimes a Super Hero could use a nice day of just wall-crawling and web-slinging.

Looking down, he thought he saw a familiar face in the shadows.

He swung over to take a closer look.

Landing on top of a building, he found himself face-to-face with the famous Avenger, Black Widow!

"Hey, Widow! Making the rounds?" asked Spidey.

At first, Black Widow looked surprised to see him, but then she smiled.

Spider-Man noticed she was staring at something. He followed her gaze to Avengers Tower in the distance. "If you're looking to head home soon, I could give you a ride," he offered. "Spidey-style."

Black Widow's smile grew. "Yes, it would be wonderful to see the Avengers again."

Again? thought Spidey. *Black Widow is an Avenger. Wouldn't she be there all the time?* But Spider-Man, not being an Avenger himself, shrugged it off.

Black Widow climbed onto Spider-Man's back. "Hold on," he said, as they swung towards Avengers Tower.

When they arrived at the tower, Spider-Man walked up to the security door and placed his hand on the scanner.

"Avengers guest, Spider-Man. Identity: confirmed. Welcome," the computerised voice said.

"What a friendly building," noted Spider-Man.

The doors opened and Spidey began to walk inside.

Black Widow started to follow, but Spider-Man stopped her. "Don't you have to check in?"

Black Widow lifted her cold eyes. Spider-Man's spider-sense tingled.

Black Widow, or whoever this imposter was, suddenly raised her arm and destroyed the scanner with her wrist blaster.

"Hey! That was a very friendly computer. You didn't have to blow it up like that, *Fake Widow*," said Spider-Man.

She was trying to get into Avengers Tower!

Spider-Man fired a web towards her, but the imposter vaulted through the air and landed gracefully on her feet behind him.

"Of course," Black Widow said, placing her hand on the security scanner.

The alarm began to sound. "Identity unknown. Intruder alert! Intruder alert!"

"Thanks for the ride," she said. "You even held the door for me. Such a gentleman."

Black Widow ran towards the open door, only to have it slam in her face!

"I guess you're not on the guest list," said Spider-Man.

Frustrated, the false Black Widow blasted the doors, but they still didn't budge. "I don't think they're going to let you in," said Spider-Man.

As Spider-Man and the imposter began to fight, a familiar-looking shield blocked one of the blasts that was about to hit Spider-Man.

Another bolt of energy came shooting down from above, landing near the imposter's feet.

Looking up, Spider-Man saw two of his Avengers friends coming to his aid: Captain America and Iron Man!

"Sorry, rules are rules. I don't want to lose my guest pass," quipped Spidey, dodging one of the phony Widow's blasts.

Iron Man dived down, but the imposter was too fast, flipping over him and grabbing onto his back.

"You shouldn't give rides to strangers, Iron Man," said the pesky villain.

With their help, Spider-Man continued to fight with the false Black Widow. She flipped and dodged Cap's shield as she fired her wrist blaster at Iron Man. "If only you had stepped aside and let me through, Spider-Fool."

Suddenly, Captain America's shield flew from behind and struck the imposter in the knees, knocking her to the ground with a thud.

Swinging into action, Spider-Man quickly webbed the evildoer's hands together, jamming the wrist blasters.

"I think it's time we find out who is behind the Black Widow mask," said Spidey.

Spider-Man pulled on the imposter's hair, but instead of a wig coming off in his hands, the foe's entire body changed! Where Black Widow had been, there now lay the pale-faced villain Chameleon!

He was a master of disguise, and his suit gave him the ability to take on the form of anyone.

"I thought Black Widow was looking a little pale today," said Spidey.

"And you nearly fell for it, too," the Chameleon snarled.

As Iron Man flew away with the Chameleon, Spider-Man turned to Captain America. "I hope this doesn't mean I'm banned from Avengers Tower for life."

Cap laughed. "Spider-Man, if you hadn't made sure that imposter followed the rules, the Chameleon would have been able to sneak in. You're always welcome here, son."

Spider was relieved. "Good, can we go inside now? Avengers Tower has the best video games and snacks in town."

The Spot
Jonathan Ohnn

The Spot is a scientist named Jonathan Ohnn who can summon big black spots. He can walk into one spot and exit from another! He can also stick his hand through a spot to attack Spider-Man, or steal things!

- Height: 5' 10"
- Occupation: Thief
- Received spots and powers by inadvertently visiting the spotted dimension when attempting to mimic portals utilised by the hero Cloak
- Can teleport using his spots, which can be suspended in midair
- Scientist specialising in physics
- Cannot throw an unlimited number of space warps as they are drawn from his own body

Seeing Spots

"My treat," she said.

Before Peter could argue, a strange black circle appeared below Gwen's purse. The friends were shocked when a white arm covered in black spots came shooting out of the hole. It grabbed Gwen's purse! Another circle appeared above them. Inside, a man's head appeared.

A menacing voice erupted from the circle. "What a lovely bag. I'm sorry, but I don't believe there will be any hot dogs today."

It was a wonderfully sunny day. Peter Parker and Gwen Stacy were strolling through Central Park, about to buy some delicious hot dogs.

"Ketchup, mustard and relish?" asked Peter.

"You know me too well, Parker," said Gwen, smiling.

Peter reached into his pocket to pay for the hot dogs when Gwen reached for her purse.

As suddenly as they appeared, the thief and his black circles disappeared. Gwen was shocked. Peter's eyes narrowed. He was not going to let some freaky villain ruin his perfect day with Gwen.

"Wait here!" exclaimed Peter. Before Gwen could say anything, Peter bolted out of sight.

Peter found an alley and changed into his Spider-Man suit to chase down the thief. He was a robber called the Spot. Swinging high, Spidey looked out over the streets of New York for signs of the criminal.

"Ha! I *spot* you!" he chuckled as he saw black circles appear beside another potential victim.

He swung off to face his foe. Spider-Man managed to web the purse before the Spot could snatch it.

"Spider-Man! I've been waiting to run into you," the Spot said. "Over and over."

Suddenly, black circles appeared all around Spidey. Out of them came fists, hitting Spider-Man as the Spot appeared and reappeared in different places. The villain was so fast that even Spider-Man's spider-sense couldn't keep up.

Spider-Man fell, beaten by the Spot. The teleporting villain appeared over him, laughing.

"Better luck next time, Bug-Brain!" the Spot taunted, vanishing into thin air.

Feeling woozy, Spidey realised he was going to need some help defeating this new menace.

Fortunately, he knew just who to call.

"Cloak! Dagger! Man, am I glad to see you guys," said Spider-Man, as he entered the church. He quickly filled them in on his encounter with the Spot.

"I need your help." Spidey turned to Cloak. "I know you're used to popping in and out of thin air, too."

"I have felt someone tapping into my teleportation force recently," noted Cloak. "It seems this Spot and I share a connection through multiple dimensions."

Spider-Man swung to an abandoned church, hoping this was still the place his friends used as a hideout.

"If anyone can help me, it'll be these two," he muttered, knowing he was running out of options. The Spot was going to be hard to defeat.

Although they had only teamed up a few times before, and one of the two could be kind of creepy, Spider-Man knew he could trust this duo to help him get the job done.

When the trio reappeared, they found themselves in the Spot's secret hideout. It was filled with all the stolen purses, jewels and other items the thief had taken on his crime spree.

"Spider-Man! How did you find me here? And who are these freaks?" the Spot asked, shocked.

Spider-Man just smiled. "Looks like you're not the only disappearing act in town, Spot."

The Spot tore the teleporting discs off of his suit, threw them around the room and started to dive into them. He was ready to attack! But this time, the good guys were ready, too.

That gave Dagger an idea. "If we can follow the energy Cloak is feeling, it could lead us to the Spot. Then my light daggers could help trap him there by draining his energy.

With the plan set, the heroes dived into the darkness of Cloak's cape and disappeared.

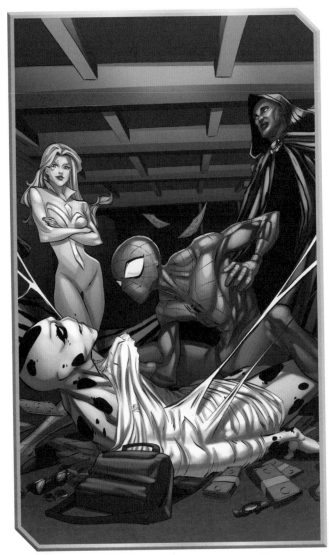

Dagger chuckled at Spidey's bad joke, while Cloak's icy stare never wavered. Their plan worked!

The Spot's thieving days were over.

The heroes helped return the stolen items. As the pile grew smaller, Spidey recognised one of the purses and grabbed it.

"Not enough pockets in your suit?" asked Dagger, with a wink.

"Hey, bad jokes are my thing," replied Spider-Man.

Then, with a quiet whoosh, Cloak whisked Dagger and the Spot away.

Bright knives shot out of Dagger's hands and burst into the dark circles. Her illuminating power filled the darkness in which the Spot thrived.

They pushed out the Spot, cutting off his escape.

Spider-Man quickly webbed the villain before he could try his teleportation tricks again. "Hmm, looks like you're stuck. I guess you could say my webs are spot-on!"

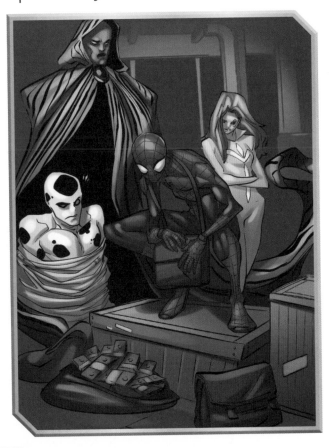

"It was incredible, Peter! Spider-Man caught the thief and brought all the stolen items back. Including my purse."

Peter blushed. "Wow, he's a real hero."

"But you are just as brave, Peter," said Gwen, hugging her friend. "Thanks for looking out for me."

Peter grinned. "I'm sorry I couldn't do more."

Back in Central Park, Peter came running back to Gwen. There was a police officer handing over her purse.

"Gwen! You got it back!" cried Peter.

"Well," said Gwen, handing the hot dog vendor money, "you certainly did enough to earn this hot dog. My treat, as promised."

"You're the best," said Peter, as he chewed. "Wow, this really hits the *spot*."

Vulture
Adrian Toomes

The Vulture is really Adrian Toomes. Toomes created an incredible flying harness that allowed him to take to the skies. Instead of using this new-found power for good, Toomes decided to use it for his own twisted purposes. He's a bad guy, is what we're saying.

- Height: 5' 11"
- Occupation: Criminal
- Inventor who created his winged harness and uses it for a life of crime
- Superhuman strength when using his mechanical harness
- Flight at high speeds with harness
- Razor-sharp talons with harness capable of tearing through steel
- Advanced engineering skills
- Member of the Sinister Six

Laundry Day

BEEP, BEEP, BEEP!
"Gahhhhh!"
Peter Parker bolted upright from his bed and stumbled around his bedroom. Still half-asleep, he promptly crashed into his nightstand and landed in a heap on the floor.

When he'd gone to bed last night, he had set his phone to its loudest alarm. He wanted to be sure to wake up on time today.

The alarm had done its job a little too well.

"Peter?" said a groggy Aunt May from the doorway. "What was that crash?"

"Um, I guess I got up on the wrong side of the bed?"

"You and me both, kiddo," said Aunt May, smiling. "But now that I'm up, how about some breakfast?"

"Can't!" exclaimed Peter. "The big Tech Expo is about to start, and—"

"Whoa, cowboy," said Aunt May. "First you need to follow me." She led Peter downstairs and into the basement.

The room was a disaster. The Parkers' washing machine had been broken for weeks, and the laundry had slowly been piling up. Every day, Peter had promised to take it to the local laundrette, but something always got in the way. More often than not, Peter was too busy fighting crime as Spider-Man.

"You can go to the Expo when all this is finished," said Aunt May.

Peter didn't have time to argue. If he was going to make it to the Tech Expo, he'd have to get his laundry done as quickly as possible. Luckily, he knew the fastest way to get around the city...

After a quick change in the alley, Peter rushed into the laundrette. He threw his first load of clothes into the machine, then ran back outside again. He was just getting started.

Three hours, four loads of laundry and way too much web-swinging later, Spidey was finally finished.

He swung back towards the Expo with his Peter Parker clothes in tow.

But just as Spidey reached the Tech Expo and got ready to change back to Peter Parker, his spider-sense went off like a siren.

As Spider-Man swung over the rooftops, his spider-sense tingled. The laundrette was just on the next block, right across the street from the Expo Centre. Spider-Man scanned the area, but from his vantage point he couldn't spot anything suspicious.

"Urgh, not him," Vulture said under his breath. The villain had spent weeks planning to rob the Expo's ticket booth. It would be easy pickings for a practised scavenger.

Unless Spider-Man got in his way.

Before he could react, Spidey felt himself fly upwards into the air. Vulture had grabbed him from behind!

"Vulture?" said Spider-Man, as they climbed further and further into the air. "Is this like an anti-Spider-Man thing, or just an anti-laundry thing? Because from the smell of your outfit..."

Vulture didn't wait for Spider-Man to finish. He spun in a barrel roll. Spidey was thrown free!

Vulture felt himself being yanked out of the air. He swung downwards and crashed through the window of a nearby apartment building. Spidey swung down and stuck to the building's brick wall.

Spider-Man peeked inside. Vulture was lying on the apartment's floor, unconscious. His Tech Expo raid certainly wasn't happening now.

Spider-Man double-tapped his web-shooter. A thin line shot out and struck the Vulture's ankle. Then he pointed his other wrist towards a nearby building and shot out another line.

Vulture tried to continue pulling Spider-Man upwards, but the Super Hero held tight to his webs.

"Urghhhh!" Spidey gave the webs one final, strong tug.

Spider-Man returned to the rooftop to grab his Peter Parker gear. With Vulture down for the count, it seemed the danger was over.

But his spider-sense didn't quite agree.

He still had time! One quick change and he could finally go to the Tech Expo.

But when he found his clothes in the wreckage of the water tower, his heart sank. Everything was soaking wet!

Spider-Man's civilian clothes tumbled in the dryer as he gazed dejectedly at the emptying-out Tech Expo across the street.

He turned his attention to a woman snapping a picture of him with her phone. "Don't tell me you've never seen a Super Hero do his laundry before," said Spidey.

The building's water tower had been damaged during his fight with Vulture. Spidey turned just in time to catch the toppling tower as waves of water cascaded over him. He gritted his teeth, holding the tower up against the water's pressure.

Spider-Man set the empty water tower back on the rooftop.

She laughed. "Somebody got up on the wrong side of the bed today."

"Yeah," sighed Spider-Man. "You don't know the half of it."

Lizard
Dr Curt Connors

The Lizard is really Dr Curt Connors, a friend of Spidey's. In an attempt to regrow his missing right arm, the scientist turned himself into a giant lizard! Which, you know, is kind of a problem.

- Height: 6' 8"
- Occupation: Professor
- Superhuman strength, stamina, agility and durability
- Resistant to conventional injuries
- Inflicts grave injuries using his savage teeth, claws and whip-like tail
- Can telepathically communicate with and control nearby reptiles
- Member of the Sinister Six

Dr Curt Connors, also known as the Lizard, was in trouble. Peter Parker knew it as soon as he saw all the pictures of the Lizard splashed across the front page of the *Daily Bugle*.

Peter also knew that his boss, J. Jonah Jameson, would be mad that Peter hadn't delivered exclusive pictures of the Lizard.

As soon as Peter walked into the *Daily Bugle* J. Jonah Jameson called him into his office.

"Parker, the Lizard is on the loose, and I need pictures," he demanded. "I want a shot for the front page. And I also want a picture of Spider-Man fighting the Lizard."

"I'm your man. I'll get you those shots," Peter told his boss.

Meanwhile, Dr Connors's wife, Martha, was very upset. She had noticed her husband mixing up a strange formula earlier that week. She knew that he was trying to create a serum that would help him grow back his missing arm, but she also knew that it came with a serious side effect. It turned Dr Connors into an evil villain called the Lizard!

Spider-Man found Martha Connors sitting on her porch, looking at a picture of her husband.

"I wish he didn't care about growing back that arm," she said, looking at Spider-Man with concern.

"Don't worry! I'll find him," said Spidey, reassuringly.

"Please hurry," said Mrs Connors. "You need to bring him to the lab and feed him the antidote."

"Got it! He won't be a lawless lizard much longer. He'll soon be back to being good old Dr Connors."

Spidey searched New York City high and low. Finally, he spotted the Lizard and chased him into an ice-cream shop, hoping to lock the cold-blooded beast in a freezer to diminish his strength. Unfortunately for Peter, the Lizard escaped!

"I'm not a fan of frozen treatsss," the Lizard hissed at Spidey.

"If you try to run from me, you're going to be on a 'rocky road'," joked Spidey.

The Lizard stomped through the streets, leaving a trail of destruction, crushing car windows and damaging shopfronts.

Spider-Man followed the Lizard as he scaled the side of the building where Dr Connors kept his lab.

"Once you go in there, I can promise you, you're not coming out," Spidey called to the angry beast.

The Lizard tried to knock Spidey down with his powerful tail, and his roars echoed through the city. People came out from the surrounding buildings and crowded around to see the excitement. Spidey was going to save the day!

Spider-Man found a window to climb through and made his way into the lab, grabbing the antidote. Suddenly, the Lizard crashed through the door, followed by a group of angry reptiles. The Lizard had given them something that let him completely control their minds. They were ready to attack!

Spider-Man looked to his left and saw a giant snake slithering towards him.

"Yikes!" shouted Spider-Man, as the monstrous snake coiled itself around his leg. Spidey quickly fired webs at the Lizard as more and more reptiles began to attack.

The Lizard dodged Spidey's webs and swung his enormous tail. Spider-Man flew through the air, crashing straight into the lab table. Spider-Man kept firing his webs, as he struggled to fight both the Lizard and the cold-blooded fiends.

Spider-Man was in full battle mode with the reptiles when the Lizard picked up a desk and threw it at him.

But it was pointless, Dr Connors had no control once the Lizard was unleashed. There was no use reasoning with a monster.

As they fought, Spidey paused to locate the antidote. The Lizard used this opportunity to unleash his final attack. He ordered the reptiles to hold Spidey down, then struck the web-slinger over and over. Spider-Man fought back hard, making sure not to bump into the antidote.

Finally, Spidey broke free, made a grab for the antidote and poured it into the Lizard's open jaws.

"Whoa!" called out Spidey. "Dr Connors, do you realise what you are doing? You have to stop the Lizard!"

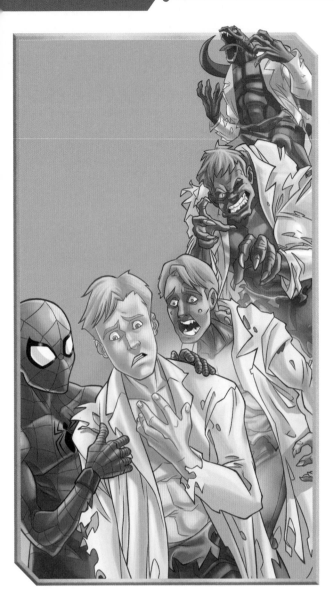

That night, Peter came home to one of Aunt May's amazing home-cooked meals.

"How was your day?" she asked. Peter didn't even know where to begin. Aunt May didn't know Peter was Spider-Man, and he certainly couldn't tell her about his fight with the Lizard. "Don't forget to save room for dessert," said Aunt May, as Peter finished his dinner. "I picked up a tub of ice cream. Your favourite, rocky road."

Within seconds, the Lizard began to morph until he slowly became Dr Connors again. Spider-Man was relieved to see the doctor's familiar face.

"Wow, what happened?" asked Dr Connors in a daze.

"It's a long story," sighed Spider-Man.

Soon, Martha Connors had her husband back, and J. Jonah Jameson had his front-page spread. Everyone was happy!

Ant-Man
Scott Lang

When told of Scott Lang's potential, Dr Hank Pym allowed him to continue to use his size-altering suit, as well as the identity Pym once battled evil under. As the astonishing Ant-Man, Scott now handles the jobs 'too small' for any other Super Hero.

Height: 6' 0"

Occupation: Adventurer

Wears a special helmet that can communicate telepathically with ants and other insects

Possesses advanced knowledge of electronics

New York City was in the middle of a heatwave. Unfortunately for Spider-Man, that wasn't going to stop the city's criminals.

"Seriously, guys? Committing crimes in a city full of Super Heroes? Not a great idea," Spider-Man said to the two bank robbers he had just webbed.

Despite the heat, Spider-Man noticed that the criminals were shivering.

"If we're going to be stuck here, how about some more webbing, huh?" one of the criminals asked, his teeth chattering.

Why were those guys acting like it's cold out? thought Spider-Man. *It's been a scorcher for weeks!*

As he swung closer to Times Square, Spidey's spider-sense began to tingle. The wind whipped around him as the temperature steadily dropped.

Just then, Spider-Man came across the source of the strange weather. A gigantic portal had opened up in the sky, sending snow flurries down upon the city.

Loki of Asgard was standing on top of a skyscraper clutching a Cosmic Cube!

"Ah, the Spider. I invite you to witness the start of my glorious reign," said Loki, proudly. "With Earth destroyed, those pesky Avengers will finally be out of my way."

"Yeah, right," said Spidey. "What are a few snowflakes going to do?"

"Just wait until you meet my friends," cackled Loki. The ground began to rumble as Loki lifted up the glowing Cosmic Cube.

Suddenly, a hoard of Frost Giants leapt from the portal into the middle of Times Square, crushing parked cars as they lumbered through the streets. The frightened tourists ran for cover as sparks from collapsing billboards rained down upon the chaotic scene.

"Meet the Frost Giants of Jotunheim," said Loki. "Now that I have the Cosmic Cube, they are under my control!"

The mindless giants paid him no attention. They were only concerned with one thing: destruction.

I don't have enough webbing left to tie up Frosty and friends, thought Spidey. *But this should slow them down.*

Spider-Man fired a web across the street. He hoped this barrier would stop the Frost Giants' destructive march.

It looked like the Frost Giants were finally going to be stopped when… *BOOM!*

Spider-Man was shocked to witness the Frost Giants step on his web barrier, causing two billboards to crash to the ground.

Spider-Man knew there was only one thing to do. He leapt into action.

THWIP!

Spidey shot his web through the air. He sailed over Times Square, straight towards one of the giants.

"Hey, Snowball! Over here!" shouted Spider-Man.

As he got closer to the giants, he narrowly missed a massive club swinging towards him.

"What do I look like, some kind of bug?" he said. Spidey looked down at his suit. "Oh, yeah, well I guess I can't really blame you."

Just then, Spider-Man spotted an Avengers Quinjet flying over.

"It's about time!" cried Spidey. He knew that with friends like Captain America, Thor, Black Widow and Iron Man on his side, Loki and his snow buddies didn't stand a chance!

Spider-Man approached the jet as it landed on a nearby rooftop. As the cargo ramp lowered, Spider-Man saw only one hero. One very small hero.

"So, what's the situation here?" said a tiny voice.

"Ant-Man!" Spider-Man was shocked as the miniature hero walked down the ramp. "Where's everyone else?"

"The Avengers are busy with Thanos," said Ant-Man. "That guy never takes a day off. Nick Fury called and said there was some trouble in the city. I'm here to back you up, pal."

"No offence, but I was expecting some bigger guns," said Spider-Man. "How are two bugs going to stop three giants?"

"Well, looks like these 'two bugs' are all New York has today," replied Ant-Man, determinedly.

Spider-Man knew Ant-Man was right. Two heads were definitely better than one. So Ant-Man grabbed on to Spidey's suit and the bug-duo swung back towards the wintry chaos.

"Look out!" exclaimed Ant-Man, as one of the Frost Giants threw a car at the approaching heroes.

"Way ahead of you!" replied Spider-Man, as he swiftly dodged the car. "But this heavy snowfall isn't making anything easier! Any ideas?"

"Well, if they want to head to Central Park, I can send in some ants to ruin their picnic," said Ant-Man, sarcastically.

"It's not warm enough for a picnic," said Spider-Man. "But wait! That gives me an idea!

How much do you know about electricity?"

"More than you, kid," replied Ant-Man. "I think I know where you're going with this."

Evading attacks from Loki's Frost Giants, Spidey swung towards Times Tower, the brightest building in the city.

As Spider-Man approached the tower, Ant-Man was able to jump just before a Frost Giant grabbed Spider-Man's webbing. The giant pulled the webs, yanking Spidey off of the tower.

"Oomph!" cried Spider-Man, as he crashed on to the hard cement.

Ant-Man knew Spider-Man couldn't hold back the giants for long. He squeezed between the bright billboards. Once inside, the small hero was able to hack into the main power grid.

"Hey, big bullies!" shouted Ant-Man. "How about turning up the heat!"

Suddenly, Times Square lit up. The light became brighter and brighter until the glare from the billboards was blinding. Hit with 161 megawatts of power, the Frost Giants quickly began to shrink until they vanished.

"Loki! Your Frost Giants should have brought sun cream," said Spider-Man, jokingly.

"Spider-Man!" roared Loki. "You did this?"

Spider-Man quickly shot a web straight towards the Asgardian villain. "I had some help. Not bad for two bugs, huh?"

With Loki blinded by webbing, Spider-Man was able to grab the Cosmic Cube and open up a portal to send Loki back to Jotunheim.

"I'll be back, Spider! I always come back!" cried Loki, as he disappeared into the portal.

"Defeated Loki, melted a bunch of Frost Giants and caused a blackout in Times Square," said Ant-Man. "I think we deserve a vacation."

"You're right," replied Spidey. "But first we have to restore power to Times Square."

"Yeah, but first… Spider!" said Ant-Man, mocking Loki. "My ants and I challenge thee to a snowball fight!"

"You're on!" replied Spider-Man.

Doctor Strange

Dr Stephen Strange

Is there a doctor in the house, or in this book? Actually, there are several! This one is Doctor Strange. He's Earth's Sorcerer Supreme, which means he defends the planet, and sometimes all reality, against magical threats. Pretty cool, right?

- Height: 6' 1"
- Occupation: Sorcerer Supreme
- Unparalleled knowledge of arcane spells and enchantments, including teleportation, astral projection and dimensional manipulation
- Vast collection of legendary artefacts, including the all-seeing eye of Agamotto, the flight-enabling cloak of levitation and the fabled book of the Vishanti
- Earth's preeminent defender against the darkness that lurks beyond

A Very Strange Night

Spider-Man has been called many things: amazing, spectacular and sensational. But today, no matter how hard Peter Parker tried, he wasn't feeling amazing, spectacular or sensational.

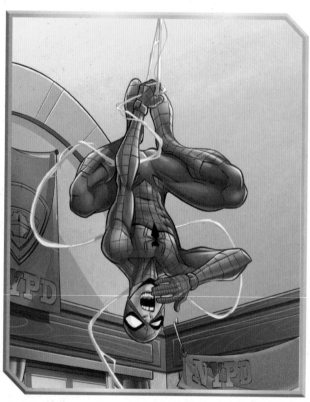

Today, Spider-Man was very, very sleepy. For the last week, Peter hadn't slept through the night. His dreams were troubling, silly and sometimes downright spooky. A week of nightmares makes for one sleepy crime-fighter.

Peter didn't think much of it, until one very long spider-yawn almost allowed Shocker to ruin the Policeman's Ball! Spidey groggily swung into action. He webbed Shocker's gauntlets before knocking the vibrating villain to the floor with a well-timed kick.

But J. Jonah Jameson, the boss of the *Daily Bugle* newspaper, was not impressed.

"Look! Not only is Spider-Man a menace, but he was sleeping on the job!" he shouted from his table as Spidey swung away.

the doctor to call…

"Doctor Strange!" said Peter, greeting his old friend. "I'm sorry to interrupt, but I've been having trouble—"

"Sleeping!" interrupted Doctor Strange, as Spider-Man entered the Sanctum Sanctorum. He had felt Peter's troubles long before Spider-Man had come to his doorstep. Doctor Strange conjured the magical Eye of Agamotto by throwing his arms out wide.

Spider-Man knew he needed help to solve his sleepy problem. He needed to see a specialist, someone who was truly an expert on dreams and the human mind. And he knew just

"The Eye of Agamotto has shown me that you've been experiencing nightmares," Strange told Peter. "And now it will show those nightmares."

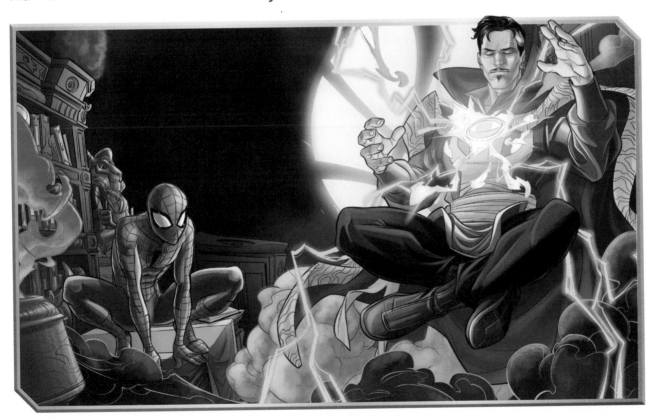

Soon, Doctor Strange was looking at Spider-Man's nightmares. In some, he was back in elementary school and forgot to wear his trousers. In others, the Sinister Six were winning every battle against him. Doctor Strange was not only able to see the future and the past, he could also see right into a person's very soul.

"Your sleep is interrupted by the supernatural, and your dreams are being invaded by the most dastardly of nocturnal threats. Your mind is plagued by the villainous Nightmare himself!" shouted Strange.

With a snap of his fingers, Strange placed Peter into a deep trance. Then, with the help of the Eye of Agamotto, he dived straight into Peter's dreams.

"The Sorcerer Supreme commands you to release your hold on this hero!" shouted Doctor Strange. But Nightmare simply laughed.

"I take power from dreams, Doctor Strange," began Nightmare, "and with a hero as strong as Spider-Man, I'll finally be great enough to defeat you!"

Peter once again found himself without his trousers on in front of his entire class. And though he was embarrassed, he was no longer alone. Doctor Strange stood tall beside him, urging him to see the nightmare for what it truly was.

"The dream is yours to control," Strange told Peter.

Peter concentrated, and the class vanished. They were replaced by the master of bad dreams, Nightmare, and his horse, Dreamstalker!

As Doctor Strange and Nightmare launched into combat, Peter knew he had to help the Sorcerer Supreme. And he realised he knew just how to do it, by using the power of imagination!

Peter thought and thought and thought, as hard as he could. To his amazement, the dream around him began to change! They weren't in Peter's school any more but on a giant chessboard, and Spider-Man was in control of the pieces.

Spidey placed move after move, defeating Nightmare's pieces, until the villain was the only one left in play.

Outnumbered, the villain retreated, finally leaving Peter Parker's mind.

"You might have won today, Strange, but you've not seen the last of me!" cried Nightmare, as he rode Dreamstalker out of Peter's mind and back to his home in the shadow realm.

"Don't worry, Nightmare, I look forward to defeating you again," replied Doctor Strange, smiling.

"It would seem Spider-Man is using the powers of his dreams against you!" declared Doctor Strange to Nightmare.

Peter woke with a start, pleased to find the good Doctor waiting with a warm cup of tea. "This is Wong's special herbal blend," said Doctor Strange. "It should calm your mind after a night like this."

After saying goodbye to his old friend, the tired hero swung home, changed into his pyjamas and slipped under the sheets. There were no monsters under the bed, and the only things in his wardrobe were his clothes and his spider-suits.

So, for the first time in what felt like weeks, Peter Parker finally got what he had been longing for – an amazing night's sleep.

Star-Lord
Peter Quill

Have you ever been to outer space? Worked in it? Joined forces with four aliens to save the galaxy? No? Same here. But Peter Quill has! As a member of the heroic Guardians of the Galaxy, Quill travels throughout space to right intergalactic wrongs.

- Height: 6' 1"
- Occupation: Space adventurer
- Half-human, half-alien
- Adept hand-to-hand combatant and marksman
- Gifted strategist, with an aptitude for thinking outside the box
- Has a unique blaster that only he can fire
- High-tech mask grants a variety of vision modes and supplies oxygen even in the vacuum of space

Great Space Expectations

Since he could remember, Peter Quill had always wanted to know about his father. One day, Peter's mother gave him a box containing delicate trinkets and pictures.

"Peter," she said, "your dad was from outer space. We fell in love and had you. Your dad had to go back home, but he left a tracker you can use to contact him… if you ever get to space."

From that day, Peter dreamt of figuring out a way to get to outer space, and to his father.

Peter studied very hard, and after many years, he became an astronaut. He was finally ready to find his dad.

Peter blasted off into the cosmos. His tracker blipped and bleeped, growing bright. On every planet he visited, Peter searched for his dad.

On one strange planet, Peter came across the Ravagers, space pirates who roamed the galaxy looking for treasure.

The Ravagers thought Peter would make a good thief and asked him to join them. Peter agreed, on the condition they helped him find his dad.

The Ravagers were kind to Peter. They even gave him a brand new ship, which he called the *Milano*. But despite the Ravagers' help, Peter still felt alone. All he wanted was to find his father.

One day, the Ravagers stopped to refuel on Knowhere, a space station that resembled a skull.

Peter heard that an intergalactic emperor was visiting the planet. He saw the crowd of people cheering on the emperor, and couldn't believe his eyes.

He pulled out an old photo he had taken with him from his special box of keepsakes, and pushed his way forward to get a closer look. The emperor was a bit older and greyer, but the face was unmistakable – Peter had found his father!

Peter had so many questions! *He needs to see me*, Peter thought. He began to climb over the protection barrier to get closer, but two royal guards yanked him away. His father had not seen him.

Dejected and alone, Peter pondered his next move. He didn't want to return to Earth. Peter enjoyed travelling the cosmos, but not with the Ravagers, who only wanted to steal. Peter wanted to discover new things.

An idea struck – he'd travel the galaxy on great adventures, making a name for himself along the way. Then maybe, just maybe, his dad would hear of this space adventurer known throughout the galaxy as… Star-Lord!

As a young girl, Gamora had been taken in by the most feared super villain in the universe: Thanos! He had raised Gamora and another girl, Nebula, to be dangerous warriors.

While Nebula liked to fight, Gamora wanted to help others. She ran away from her evil family in search of something better.

Star-Lord tracked down Gamora, and the two bonded instantly.

She understood Peter's quest to find his family… and his feelings of loneliness.

On his intergalactic travels, Star-Lord learnt of a great warrior named Gamora.

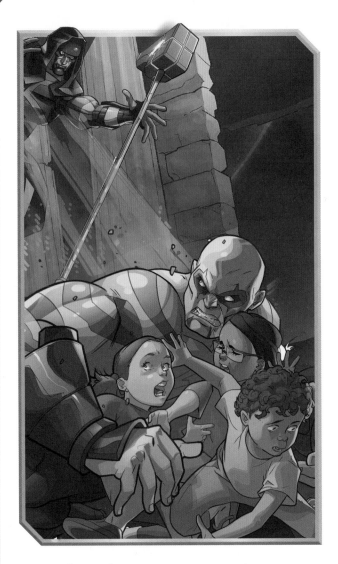

The group's next stop was Planet X. Drax had told Star-Lord about the planet's sprawling forests filled with mythical tree-like beings. Star-Lord thought there might be an exciting discovery for him there. But the beings all shied away from the trio, except for one friendly tree named Groot.

Groot's life on Planet X was pleasant but boring – he craved excitement and adventure, just like Star-Lord! Groot asked to join the group on their journey, and Star-Lord welcomed him aboard the *Milano*.

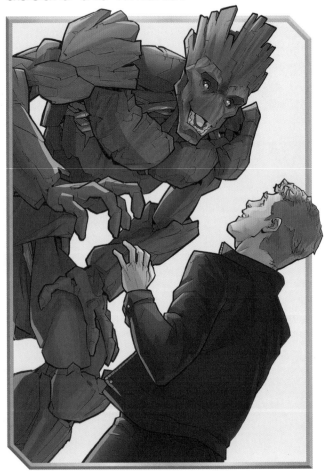

Before long, Star-Lord and Gamora encountered a great warrior named Drax the Destroyer.

Drax had lost his family long ago, and travelled the galaxy fighting against injustice, always standing up for the weak. He agreed to join Star-Lord and Gamora, because he also knew what it felt like to be without a family.

Drax would never admit it, but he was lonely, too.

The group then travelled to a planet called Halfworld, where they met a fierce-looking raccoon standing on top of a pile of defeated aliens.

But this was no ordinary raccoon. His name was Rocket, and a team of scientists had given him great intelligence. Star-Lord thought adding Rocket to the group, with his resourcefulness and smarts, would help them along their adventures, and Rocket was all alone – so Star-Lord invited Rocket aboard their ship.

The raccoon accepted his offer, excited for the adventures and escapades that lay ahead.

The team was now ready for greatness. But just as Star-Lord boarded their ship, his father's tracker began to blink. His dad was on planet Halfworld!

Star-Lord and the group followed the tracker, and, when Star-Lord saw a figure in the distance, he immediately recognised the emperor he'd seen so long ago on Knowhere. This time, he made sure his dad noticed him.

Star-Lord was happy he'd at last located his father, but he realised he'd already found exactly what he had been searching for, a family. He'd found it with Gamora, Drax, Groot and Rocket.

They all agreed to continue to travel the galaxy together.

The Guardians of the Galaxy were officially born!

Groot
He is Groot

This is Groot! He's a tree. Well, sort of. He comes from Planet X, where a race of tree-like beings dwell. The only thing Groot can say is "I am Groot". At least, that's what it sounds like to us. But to somebody who speaks Groot's language, it can mean practically anything!

- Height: Variable
- Occupation: Space adventurer
- Member of a tree-like alien race
- Superhuman strength
- Ability to quickly regenerate after enduring physical damage
- Plant-like form enables him to grow or reshape his limbs and root himself in place for enhanced stability
- Can emit glowing spores
- Only says the phrase "I am Groot"

The Groot Escape

ZAP! BANG! BOOM!
The planet Xandar was under attack from Kree soldiers. The Guardians of the Galaxy had called on the Avengers for help. But even so, the Super Heroes were outnumbered.

"Retreat!" cried Star-Lord. But when he tried to fire up his starship, the *Milano*, the engines wouldn't start.

"We'll hold them off," said Captain America. "Rocket, Groot, you go fix the ship!"

"Okay, you heard the man," said Rocket. "I'll go check on the thrusters. You stay here and wait for my signal."

Groot gave a tiny salute.
"I am Groot!"

Suddenly, Groot spotted three tiny Orloni creatures sneaking onto the ship. If there was one thing Groot couldn't stand, it was Orloni.

"Rawwwr!" cried Groot, who leapt after the pests. They scattered, and two of them fled into the cargo hold.

Groot rushed into the hold, where Iron Man was under attack from a Kree fighter. Groot ignored them and chased after an Orloni. *CRASH!*

He knocked over a weapons rack, causing one of the blasters to fire and knock down the Kree soldier.

"What's all the ruckus about?" asked Rocket, hanging his head down from the engine room.

"Alien guy almost had me," replied Iron Man. "But tiny tree dude got him!"

"Way to go, pal!" said Rocket.

Groot was surprised. He looked over at the fallen Kree soldier and was pleased to see that one of the Orloni had somehow been trapped in a crate beneath him.

Groot beamed with pride. "I am Groot."

As the friends walked along, an Orloni ran past them and scampered straight into the main engine pipe.

Without a moment's hesitation, Groot chased after it.

Groot chased the tiny Orloni through the pipe system. They didn't stop until the Orloni screeched to a dead end. But it wasn't a dead end at all, it was a mass of old sludge clogging the pipes.

Groot waved goodbye as Iron Man jumped back into the fight outside.

"There isn't enough power getting to the thrusters," said Rocket. "Let's go check what's blocking the pipes."

The terrified Orloni kept ramming into the sludge until it burst right through. Suddenly, Groot felt a deep rumble and heard Rocket's voice calling through the pipes.

"You did it," cried Rocket.

Groot felt the engines heating up as he sped back down the pipes. Rocket caught him as he slid out through the grate, then he called out to the other heroes.

"Okay, we're ready, now let's get out of here!"

Star-Lord set the thrusters to full power, and the *Milano* took off with a jolt, dodging fire from the Kree army as it sped into outer space.

"Great job back there, Rocket," said Captain America. "You got the ship working just in time."

"Don't thank me," replied Rocket, lifting up Groot. "This little guy was the one who risked his life to unclog the engine."

"I am Groot," beamed Groot. He was happy that he had helped his friends, but he couldn't stop thinking about that Orloni who escaped.

Where could that little critter be?

Rocket
Not a Raccoon

If you travel the galaxy, you'll never meet anyone like Rocket! That's because only Rocket is like Rocket! That makes sense, right? Anyway, Rocket was kind of like a raccoon, we guess, until a team of scientists experimented on the little guy. He has all the abilities of a raccoon – a heightened sense of sight, sound and smell – but he was also given increased intelligence. That Rocket is one smart creature!

- Height: 3' 0"
- Occupation: Space adventurer
- Master pilot, engineer, marksman and weapons specialist
- Genetically and cybernetically enhanced
- Highly agile
- Mechanical genius (especially engineering, vehicles and heavy munitions)
- Tough talker

"**Y**OU LOST WHAT?!" Peter Quill, also known as Star-Lord, shouted at Rocket, his small, furry, not-so-cuddly shipmate and fellow Guardian of the Galaxy.

Rocket rolled his eyes. "It's called the Singularity Instigator. What do you care, Star-Bored? It's my stuff."

"We're the *Guardians* of the Galaxy, not the *Accidental Destroyers* of the Galaxy!" cried Quill. "That thing can create black holes from radiation!"

"Don't get all wound up," groaned Rocket. "Look, I got a tracker on it. We'll have it back before you're done complaining."

In fact, Star-Lord wasn't done complaining, but when he turned to scold his raccoon-like teammate again, Rocket was on his way to Earth… and he'd taken Groot with him.

Rocket and Groot followed the tracker to a remote desert, where they ran into none other than the Incredible Hulk!

"Oh, great," muttered Rocket. "It just had to be the Hulk."

"I am Groot!" cried Groot, wrapping his branches around the green giant before Rocket even had time to think.

"Hey!" protested Hulk. "Off Hulk! Off!"

"I am Groot!"

"Well, okay," said Rocket. "I guess we could try talking to him first."

The duo cautiously approached Hulk.

"Why you tie Hulk up?" the green giant asked, more confused than angry.

"Because you took our Singularity Instigator!" cried Rocket.

Now Hulk was even more confused. "Hulk does not know what fur-alien talking about," he said. "Hulk busy looking for enemy."

With the Hulk all wrapped up, Rocket and Groot turned away to plan. But no sooner had they left the Hulk's side than he burst out of his restraints with ease! Rocket turned to Groot, frustrated. "We need an actual plan here!"

Rocket and Groot followed their new ally to a nearby ridge. Down in the crater, the Singularity Instigator was in fact there, in the hands of none other than the archenemy Hulk had been searching for, the Leader!"

"Hey, Ginormous Head," called out Rocket. "That's mine. What are you planning to do with it?"

The Leader smiled. "Why, I intend to hold the world hostage, or I'll create a black hole and destroy the entire planet, of course!"

"Well, we're looking for something, too," said Rocket. "Maybe we could help each other out."

The Guardians filled the Avenger in on what had brought them to Earth.

After a few minutes of Rocket describing the Singularity Instigator, Hulk's eyes widened in recognition.

"Hulk see garbage machine," said Hulk. "Follow Hulk."

Rocket grinned. "That's right, buddy. You help us, we'll help you track down this enemy of yours."

Hulk grimaced. "Found enemy," he growled. "And dumb machine."

"Hulk, you got a cool battle cry or anything we can use?" asked Rocket.

"Yes," said Hulk, as he lunged towards the Leader, yelling, "Hulk smash!"

The trio jumped into battle against the villain. Groot tried to grab the Leader, but his opponent had a hidden force-field generator that caused Groot's hands to splinter on impact. Rocket's rifle blasts bounced off the same powerful force-field.

THOOM!

The Hulk landed right behind the Leader. But the villain was ready for him with a powerful blaster pulse.

Rocket and Groot exchanged a look, it was up to them now.

"Groot, use our playbook – Cage Formation!" cried Rocket.

Groot's twig-like fingers began to extend longer and longer, branching off and twisting into a makeshift cage that encircled the villain. The Leader was so surprised, he didn't notice one of Groot's twigs was hiding an anti-gravity lifter… until Groot slapped the device directly on the villain's giant forehead!

"Bye-bye!" cried Rocket, as he waved at the Leader, who had now taken to the skies, dropping the Singularity Instigator on the ground in his wake.

"Hulk thanks friends," said Hulk, as he hugged Rocket and Groot. "You helped Hulk fight big-headed enemy."

Rocket struggled to catch his breath. "And you helped us find our lost Singularity Instigator, Hulk. We'll be taking it back into space now."

"I am Groot," said Groot.

"Okay, okay," said Rocket, rolling his eyes. "We'll put it in a safe place this time. Somewhere no one will ever find it. Like Quill's underwear drawer. No one ever goes in there for anything anyway!"

Drax
The Destroyer

Drax the Destroyer is a fearsome warrior with super-strength. He joined Peter Quill's team to help keep the galaxy safe. Fierce and powerful, Drax is great to have in any battle.

- Height: 6' 5"
- Occupation: Space adventurer
- Superhuman strength and durability
- Fuelled by revenge for his family
- Ferocious hand-to-hand combatant
- Highly skilled with blades and other close-combat gear
- Direct but rough-edged in communication

Mixed Signals from Knowhere

"I'm not scared of you," scoffed Star-Lord.

Just then, a distress signal was picked up by the *Milano*.

Phew! Saved by the bell, thought Star-Lord.

"It's coming from somewhere on Knowhere," said Rocket.

"Well, is it somewhere or nowhere?" frowned Drax.

The Guardians of the Galaxy had just landed on the space station called Knowhere when an argument erupted between Star-Lord and Drax.

"You never have my back," shouted Star-Lord.

"Why would I have your back?" cried Drax. "You are being ridiculous. Leave me alone. Don't think I won't fight you."

Star-Lord's hot temper flared. "Rocket just said, it's somewhere on Knowhere, obviously."

Drax was furious, but he knew they had a job to do.

As soon as the Guardians stepped off the ship, they were shocked to discover Iron Man firing deadly blasts at a building.

"Iron Man might be our friend," yelled Star-Lord, "but we can't let him destroy the space station."

At that moment, a green blur slammed into Iron Man.

"Hulk smash!" roared Hulk, as he squished Iron Man into the ground.

"I believe you've met Hulk?" said Thor.

The heroes were dodging Iron Man's fiery blasts, when a voice boomed overhead. "Need a hand?"

It was the mighty Thor, who was also responding to the distress signal.

Thor swung his hammer to deflect one of Iron Man's powerful blasts.

"What are you waiting for?" yelled Rocket.

"You'll see," said Thor, "in three… two… one."

"I am Groot," whispered Groot to Rocket.

"You're one to talk," replied Rocket, who was the only one who ever understood what Groot was saying. "I'd say you're very weird-looking yourself."

Star-Lord turned to Drax. "Now let's settle our fight!"

"Guys!" said Gamora. "One of you needs to end this now."

"It takes two to tango," replied Star-Lord, who would only apologise if Drax did so, as well.

"I will never dance with you!" shouted Drax.

"Wait, Drax," said Gamora. "You're misunderstanding what Star-Lord means when—"

"Um, friends," interrupted Thor, as he received an urgent call through his communicator. "I think you'll want to hear this. It's Tony Stark!"

"But if that's Tony Stark, then who's in the Iron Man suit?" asked Gamora, pointing to the figure beneath Hulk's hand.

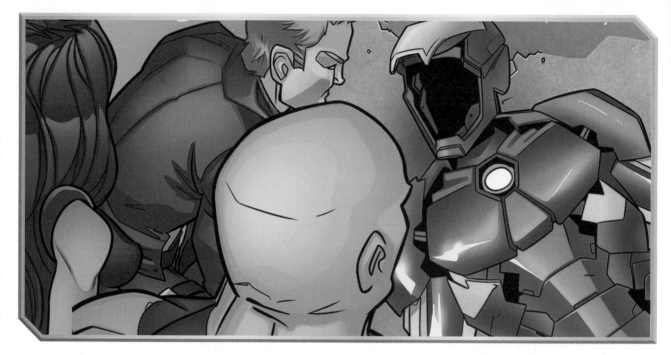

"Only one way to find out," said Star-Lord. He bent down to open Iron Man's helmet. The heroes gasped. There was no one inside.

"The suit's empty!" cried Star-Lord.

"That's what I was going to tell you," explained Tony Stark through Thor's communicator. "That is the spare drone I keep on the *Milano* for deep-space missions. JARVIS just told me that it's malfunctioning."

"You could say that..." said Star-Lord.

"Let's get this suit back to Tony for repair," said Thor.

"That's not the only thing that needs repairing," said Gamora, turning to Star-Lord. "Your friendship needs repairing, too.

Drax thinks you mean he literally needs to have your back."

Drax looked confused. "Your back is small and weak."

Star-Lord hung his head in shame. "Sorry, man. It's a figure of speech. I don't really think you need my back. I guess we were all a little mixed up today."

Nebula
Daughter of Thanos

Nebula is a cunning warrior. Part machine, Nebula's strength and speed have been increased, making her a real threat to the Guardians of the Galaxy. She would destroy them just to get at her sister, Gamora.

- Height: 5' 11"
- Occupation: Mercenary
- Merciless space pirate
- Adopted daughter of Thanos and adopted sister of Gamora
- Heightened strength, agility, durability and reflexes due to extensive cybernetic augmentation
- Skilled physical combatant, with expertise in a variety of advanced weaponry
- Cunning tactician, manipulator and strategist
- Seeks to achieve victory and power by any means

"Oh, boy," said Rocket. "Nova Corps wants to board our ship!"

The Guardians agreed to let the Nova Corps on board.

I just wish Nebula had joined us," said Gamora, sighing. She and Star-Lord were piloting the *Milano* through a quiet night in the galaxy, waiting for their next big mission. "She's always so stubborn."

Just then, the ship's emergency light began to blink. The Guardians all gathered around Star-Lord and Gamora.

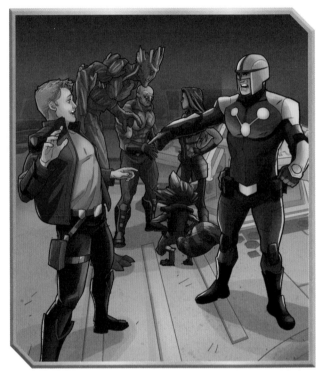

"Where is it?" asked the Nova Corps officer in a thunderous, booming voice once he'd boarded the *Milano*. "Where's the Deep Freeze?"

"Whoa, whoa, whoa," protested Star-Lord. It appeared as though the Nova Corps had been robbed, and they were angry. "The deep what? Why would we have had something to do with it?"

The officer glared at him. "It wasn't supposed to leave Nova Corps yet. Now that it's been in an insecure environment it'll need to be destroyed."

Star-Lord gave a winning smile. "Listen, we had nothing to do with it, honest. In fact, as a show of good faith, we'll even help you find the perp!"

The officer played the Guardians footage of a cloaked figure in the Nova lab.

"Oh, I know just who that is," said Gamora, her eyes darkening.

Gamora started to set the *Milano* on a course for Morag, home to an underground market for stolen goods. That's where they'd find Nebula, and the Deep Freeze.

Just when Gamora thought Nebula might have changed, her adoptive sister was getting into trouble again. Growing up, the super villain Thanos had inspired competition between the two sisters by forcing them to fight each other. But that was no excuse for living a life of crime. Gamora would have to stop Nebula, by any means necessary.

Once the Nova Corps officer left the *Milano*, the Guardians travelled to Morag. As soon as they landed, Gamora ran off ahead of the rest of the Guardians.

She navigated the streets until she spotted an old wooden door with strange markings on it.

Gamora descended a creaky stairway into the darkness below. At the bottom of the stairs, a tunnel branched off in two directions. Gamora looked one way, then the other. Suddenly, she spotted a crumpled object a few feet down the tunnel to her right. The material was a discarded cloak, the same one she'd seen Nebula wearing in the security video. She was on the right track!

"Is someone there?" a voice rang out down the tunnel. "Why don't you quit skulking in the shadows and join me?"

With the element of surprise up in smoke, Gamora entered the room to find Nebula standing in a corner holding a strange-looking device.

"Ah, Gamora," said Nebula, "what an unpleasant surprise."

"Sister," said Gamora. "Nova Corps is missing a very specific piece of technology. Apparently releasing it into the environment before it's ready could be super dangerous." She gestured towards the object Nebula held in her hands.

Nebula smirked. "What, this old thing? Nope. It was a gift," she said with a grin.

Gamora gritted her teeth. "Give. It. To. Me."

Nebula's eyes narrowed. "Make me."

Gamora dived at Nebula, knocking the Deep Freeze out of her sister's hand as she kicked, punched and clawed. It was like no time had passed between the two as they fought, much like they had as children.

And just like when they were young, only one could be the winner.

"Enough!" bellowed Nebula, gaining hold of the Deep Freeze once more. She pressed a button on the device and Gamora froze.

In horror, Gamora watched her arm lower itself and drop her sword. Gamora was powerless to respond. Nebula seemed to be controlling her body with the device!

"Clever isn't it?" said Nebula. "They're doing all sorts of wonderful things with technology at Nova Corps these days. Imagine all the trouble I can cause now!"

Suddenly, Star-Lord burst into the room. "Not so fast! When you mess with Gamora, you mess with all of us!"

Gamora couldn't smile, but she cheered on the inside. Her friends had followed her trail and found her!

Rocket appeared holding a giant cannon. Then Drax came in. He looked over at Gamora and said, "Why is she just standing there?"

"I am Groot?" a deep voice boomed out. Groot lumbered through the doorway.

"No, pal," said Rocket, "I don't think she turned into a tree."

"Okay," Star-Lord said to Nebula, "we can do this the easy way, or the fun way."

Nebula grinned. "Let's have some fun, shall we?"

Just then, Nebula pressed a button on the device and thrust it in the Guardians' direction. The whole team froze where they were. Nebula turned back to the Guardians, and as she was distracted Rocket felt his hand was still free. He shot his cannon, destroying the Nova Corps device just as the officer had instructed.

As the device shattered, the Guardians were released from Nebula's hold. The Guardians flexed their limbs as they regained control of their bodies.

Gamora picked up her sword and turned to face Nebula. But her sister was already on the move.

The Guardians followed Nebula into the tunnels. Gamora was the first to catch up with her sister, the thief.

"You want us to hang back while you take her?" Star-Lord asked Gamora.

Gamora had never thought she would truly turn against family. But, she realised her real family was standing right in front of her. And she needed their help to defeat her adoptive sister.

She shook her head. "No," she said. "We're a team, let's do this together."

The team nodded at Gamora as they headed towards Nebula. With some help from Drax and the rest of the group, Gamora propelled towards Nebula and knocked her off her feet.

The Guardians watched as Gamora handcuffed Nebula. "Now you're the one that can't move sister," she said smugly.

Gamora turned to the Guardians. "You know, we're not just a team. You guys are also my family."

Gamora couldn't be sure, but she thought she caught Star-Lord blushing.

Gamora

The Deadliest Woman in the Galaxy

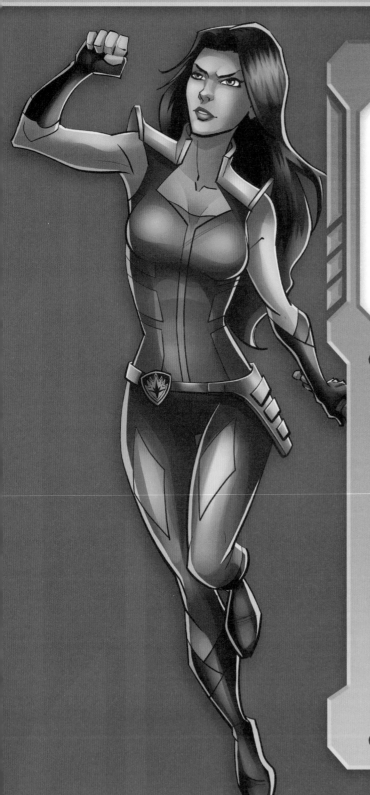

If there's anyone more dangerous in the galaxy than Gamora, we haven't met them! When Gamora was just a little girl, the Mad Titan, Thanos, came to her planet and wiped out her people. He 'saved' Gamora and trained her to fight better than anyone so he could use her to fight his battles.

- Height: 5' 9"
- Occupation: Space adventurer
- Adopted daughter of Thanos. Raised with her adopted sister, Nebula
- Strength, agility, physical conditioning and healing rate heightened by cybernetic implants and genetic alteration
- Unparalleled warrior, master of hand-to-hand combat
- Experience in virtually all known martial arts
- Proficient in a wide variety of weaponry
- Highly skilled in the art of subterfuge

"Yeah, Quill," added Rocket. "I'm trying to concentrate here."

"I am Groot!" said Groot, dropping his playing cards in annoyance.

"**A**nybody know what time it is?" asked Star-Lord.

"Not again!" groaned Rocket.

"This guy gets it," said Star-Lord. "It's mix-tape time!"

"Peter, please," said Gamora.

"Make it stop!" shouted Drax. "I came here for sleep, not to shake whatever a 'groove thing' is."

Peter had just found a new mix tape on one of the Guardians' missions. And while the others were trying to relax on this deserted asteroid, Star-Lord was too busy dancing to listen to them complain.

Gamora said, "Let's all just take a breath and—"

She was interrupted by a beeping noise from the *Milano*.

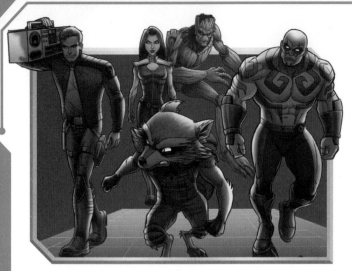

"Aw, great. The emergency beacon," grumbled Rocket. The group headed to their ship.

"Greetings, Guardians of the Galaxy," said an alien on their monitor. "The government of the planet Drakenthom would like to employ your services."

The alien explained that a band of intergalactic pirates was hiding out on Drakenthom, a planet known for its complete silence, and that the Guardians were needed to kick the pirates off Drakenthom for good.

"We'll do it!" Star-Lord agreed happily.

In no time, the Guardians had tracked down the pirates on a remote Drakenthom beach.

"Put your hands where we can see them!" Star-Lord shouted, as he dropped from the Guardians' ship. He waved his blaster in his hand.

Gamora threw Star-Lord an angry look.

"What?" asked Star-Lord.

Gamora didn't answer and just put her finger to her lips.

It was just like Star-Lord to forget the only rule of their mission.

He mouthed, "Sorry."

Then, Star-Lord studied the landscape, which was almost eerily quiet.

For wanted criminals, these pirates were following Drakenthom's silence laws to the letter.

The Guardians were overwhelmed. Star-Lord realised that without any leadership, the team was going to lose this fight, and quickly.

He was going to have to break the silence.

"Rocket, Groot! Take out the guns!" shouted Star-Lord. "Gamora! Drax! Force them back!"

Before he could think too much about it, Star-Lord found himself leaping out of the way of a laser blast.

The pirates began firing at them just as the rest of the Guardians landed on the beach. Surprisingly, their lasers were as silent as the pirates themselves.

The plan worked! But just as the Guardians trapped the pirates in one of the beach's many caves, the ground began to rumble and shake.

A large dragon-like beast suddenly burst out of the caves. And it didn't look happy.

"Ahh!!!" cried Star-Lord, as he ran for cover. The dragon followed him, shooting white-hot flames out of its mouth.

"Quill!" yelled Gamora.

The dragon turned its head towards her.

"The thing's attracted to sound," called Rocket, as he, too, sought cover from the flames erupting from the beast's mouth. "And Captain Blabbermouth there woke it up!"

Drakenthom's need for complete silence suddenly made sense.

Without speaking, Gamora ran towards the Guardians' ship. She had an idea.

You like sound, buddy, she thought to herself as she reached the *Milano. I'll give you sound.*

Gamora was running out of time. But then her eyes landed on exactly what she needed. Gamora grinned. *Bingo.*

Meanwhile, the dragon had cornered Star-Lord. It snapped its massive jaws at the hero and began to advance.

The Guardians took advantage of the dragon's distraction and rushed back into their ship. As the *Milano* took off, the strange beast followed close behind.

It seemed that not only could the dragon survive in space, but he could also somehow hear the music in the Guardians' ship. And he liked what he was hearing.

The Guardians led the dragon all the way back to the deserted asteroid where they had received the call from Drakenthom. Gamora descended from the *Milano* and gently placed the boombox in the centre of a large crater.

Then suddenly, it stopped. Gamora had Star-Lord's boombox raised over her head, playing his new mix tape.

As Gamora walked back to the *Milano*, Star-Lord looked longingly out the ship's window at the beast. It had curled around his boombox and fallen asleep!

The Guardians' ship flew off into deep space.

"I'm really going to miss that tape," mumbled Quill, sadly.

Gamora looked at him sympathetically. But she didn't reply.

In fact, no one did.

No one was arguing.

No one was even speaking. The Guardians of the Galaxy were too busy enjoying some well-earned peace and quiet.

Captain Marvel
Carol Danvers

Carol Danvers was one of the best pilots the U.S. Air Force ever had! But she didn't want to just fly planes, she wanted to soar into the stars! Carol would one day get her wish, just not quite the way she expected.

- Height: 5' 11"
- Occupation: Alpha Flight Leader
- Superhuman strength, stamina and durability
- Can fly at high speeds and project intense energy blasts
- Can tap into and absorb different forms of energy, transforming into a powerful alternate form known as Binary
- Experienced espionage agent and hand-to-hand combatant

Full Force

arol Danvers was having a blast as her jet soared through the clouds above a classified airfield somewhere in the United States. She was an ace fighter pilot for the U.S. Air Force, and it was no secret that she was the best of the best.

Carol worked hard protecting her country from every type of threat. She fought to save civilian lives and protect her fellow soldiers.

The United States was safe thanks to Carol Danvers.

Eventually, NASA heard about Carol Danvers and her stellar military record. They recruited her to be their head of security,

protecting the United States from cosmic threats.

In her new position, Carol learned not only that aliens were real, but that some of them were bent on destroying Earth!

One of those alien races was the Kree Empire. NASA was concerned that their endless galactic wars were making Earth vulnerable to alien attacks. So Carol invited the Kree leaders to NASA Headquarters. She knew she needed to form an alliance with the Kree. The safety of the whole planet was at stake.

During the meetings, Carol became friends with the Kree dignitaries, especially their central leader, Captain Mar-Vell. However, that would not last long. One of the Kree, the evil Yon-Rogg, did not want peace. So he came up with a plan.

Yon-Rogg captured Carol along with a powerful alien device he had taken from the Kree ship.

It didn't take long for Captain Mar-Vell to find them! During the battle, the alien device blew up, creating a massive explosion that engulfed everyone.

Even Carol Danvers.

Weeks later, Carol began to feel strange. One night, she started feeling dizzy until suddenly her world went black. The next thing Carol knew, she was floating! She felt powerful and could create sparkling energy with her hands. Carol Danvers had transformed into a superhuman. Eventually, she would become the Super Hero known as Captain Marvel!

In the aftermath, Carol escaped unhurt but Yon-Rogg was never seen again. Captain Mar-Vell and his fellow Kree left Earth to continue their galactic wars. Although the peace mission was a failure, Carol knew that working with the Kree, and trying to negotiate a peace, had been the right thing to do.

The explosion had awakened Carol's super-powers! She started to test them and found she could fly through the air just by thinking it! By tightening her fists, she could send blasts of powerful photon energy. She could even absorb different types of energy and use it to enhance her already powerful superhuman abilities.

Captain Marvel had become stronger, faster and virtually indestructible.

As a Super Hero, Captain Marvel was able to do things she'd only dreamt of as a pilot. She took to the skies, exploring the far reaches of space, always using her powers for good.

Along the way, she made new friends and new enemies. But in the end, something always pulled her back home to Earth.

As leader of Alpha Flight, Captain Marvel was able to prevent a massive attack from an evil alien army, the Chitauri.

Under Captain Marvel's direction, her amazing team created a giant shield that protected the planet from the alien's weaponry. The Chitauri were defeated and Earth was safe once again!

Captain Marvel's military training had made her Earth's fiercest protector. Whether it was a meteor hurtling through the planet's atmosphere, or a galactic council meeting, Captain Marvel was always ready to protect and represent Earth.

After saving the world many times, Captain Marvel was recruited to lead a special space programme – Alpha Flight. The purpose of this new organisation was to be Earth's first line of defence against alien threats.

In addition to working for Alpha Flight, Captain Marvel also teamed up with other Super Heroes to defend the world. One of those teams was Earth's Mightiest Heroes, the Avengers! Their missions took Captain Marvel all over the world and into the cosmos. But when the job was done, Captain Marvel always returned home to Earth, and her Alpha Flight crew. Whether flying solo or with her fellow heroes, Captain Marvel was a force to be reckoned with!

Gamora! What was the Guardians of the Galaxy warrior doing out here all alone? And who, or what, was she fighting?

Suddenly, Gamora's opponent appeared through the fog – it was Thanos!

Captain Marvel was shooting through space when she intercepted a distress signal. It led her to a strange purple planet.

The surface was covered in a thick fog. Through a break in the fog, she saw a green-skinned woman with a sword.

"Oh, boy," muttered Captain Marvel.

Up close, Gamora looked tired, like she'd been battling the giant villain for hours.

"Gamora, take a breather. I've got this," said Captain Marvel, as she leapt to help her friend, confident in her own ability to tackle such a fearsome foe.

Captain Marvel gritted her teeth, momentarily caught off guard by the Kree's surprise attack. Thanos would have to wait a little while longer.

"Captain Marvel! How did you get here? And where did that Kree come from?" asked Gamora, as she continued to fend off Thanos.

Captain Marvel used her fists to blast her opponent with a powerful energy burst, then said, "I intercepted your distress signal and came to help. As for this garbage heap, his name is Yon-Rogg." She launched a flying kick at her foe, before adding, "Let's take these bad guys down!"

Just before Captain Marvel could reach Gamora and Thanos, Yon-Rogg – one of Captain Marvel's oldest enemies – tackled her from out of nowhere!

KA-POW!

Captain Marvel's energy blast fired brightly, lighting up the surrounding fog.

SHWIIING!

Gamora's sword swung quickly. But neither enemy retreated!

"This is a nightmare," grumbled Captain Marvel, fighting off Yon-Rogg once more.

"Wait a minute, what if this place is actually Planet Nightmare?" said Gamora. "That must be where we are! It knows your worst fears and pits them against you." Her eyes widened. "That means these villains aren't real. They've been created from our own imaginations."

Captain Marvel frowned. "Real or not, how do we beat them?"

Gamora smiled. "We have to catch them off guard and give them something they won't see coming. Ready for a switch?"

Catching the bad guys by surprise, both Super Heroes quickly gained the upper hand.

But the villains were still a threat. Gamora landed a solid blow to Yon-Rogg, which stunned him, but only for a few seconds.

The dynamic duo swapped enemies. Gamora challenged Yon-Rogg, while Captain Marvel faced Thanos!

"Let's get 'em!" whooped Captain Marvel.

"Are you okay?" Gamora called out to her friend. But there was only a bright purple light coming from where Captain Marvel had stood just a moment before.

"Better than ever," replied Captain Marvel, confidently.

Yon-Rogg quickly grabbed hold of Gamora.

"That was a mistake, Kree slime," said Gamora, through gritted teeth.

Thanos wasn't beaten yet, either. He deployed his most dangerous weapon, his power-blast, which completely surrounded Captain Marvel!

Gamora turned to see a super-charged Captain Marvel. The Super Hero had absorbed all the energy of Thanos's power-blast!

"Grrraaaah!" Gamora twisted free from Yon-Rogg's grip and knocked him back with a powerful punch. The Kree from Captain Marvel's mind was defeated.

Meanwhile, Captain Marvel hurled a massive blast of energy towards Thanos. He went flying up into the sky and disappeared, finally beaten, once and for all.

"And that's how you do it," declared Captain Marvel, after the pair had won.

"Now let's hurry off this planet," said Gamora. "It's been my worst nightmare."

Captain Marvel led Gamora safely to her ship. As they said goodbye, the craft's incoming-message light started blinking.

"Gamora, come in!" cried Star-Lord over the radio. "Where have you been?"

Gamora waved at Captain Marvel and said to Star-Lord, "Oh, nowhere special. I was just helping out a friend!"

Iron Man
Tony Stark

Tony Stark is very rich and incredibly smart. He graduated from college at a young age and inherited his dad's company, Stark Industries. Now he is the Super Hero Iron Man, using his arc-reactor-powered suit to protect the innocent from harm.

- Height: 6' 1" / 6' 5" in armour
- Occupation: Inventor
- Genius-level intellect with particular aptitude in invention and engineering
- Billionaire industrialist
- Wears modular arc-reactor-powered Iron Man armour granting superhuman strength and durability
- Armoured suit grants ability to fly and project repulsor blasts
- Armour is outfitted with complex tech, including a cutting-edge artificial intelligence, sophisticated sensor systems and other gadgetry

The Invincible Iron Man

As a boy, Tony Stark dreamt about how technology could change the world for the better.

Tony was just nineteen years old when he started designing cutting-edge technology for his family's company, Stark Industries. But to create, Tony would need money, space and resources. The U.S. Army was happy to give him everything he needed as long as Tony invented stronger weapons for their soldiers.

The army asked Tony, who was already the head of Stark Industries, to teach their soldiers how to use his weapons to keep evil forces at bay. Tony was still young, and was excited to show that he could handle such an important task.

KABOOM!

Suddenly, while Tony was in a foreign land, an attack broke out! He was blasted off his feet and felt a sharp pain in his chest before slamming into the ground. Everything went black.

When Tony woke up, he was surprised to see a smiling face looking down at him. The man's name was Dr Ho Yinsen.

He told Tony there was shrapnel lodged very close to his heart.

Yinsen had created a powerful magnet that kept the shrapnel in place, preventing it from killing Tony.

Suddenly, several warlords barged into the cave where Tony and Yinsen were trapped. They demanded that Tony and Yinsen build powerful weapons for them. If Tony and Yinsen didn't deliver what they wanted, they would be prisoners forever!

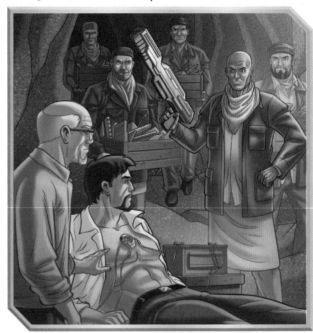

The two scientists decided they would give these warlords exactly what they wanted, but with a twist! They set to work right away, using the tools and equipment the warlords had brought them.

It took weeks, but both men worked very hard, because they were eager to be set free. Large pieces of grey metal were coming together, they had a power source to run their creation, and when their time was up, they put their plan into action!

As the warlords approached, Tony strapped himself into his weapon. It wasn't some kind of ray gun or rocket, it was a powered-up battle suit! Yinsen took cover as Tony, now an iron man, smashed through the prison door.

The warlords' weapons hardly made a dent in the grey armour! Iron Man was invincible! He charged towards the warlords and they fled in fear.

Tony made it out of the cave, but Yinsen didn't. The guilt weighed heavily on Tony's mind, but there was something else. Tony had a realisation that shook him to his core. Many of the weapons he had destroyed were those he had created himself!

Tony felt ashamed that his work was being used by warlords. He also felt something new. There was just a spark of it, a hint of pride that he had taken weapons away from bad people.

But escaping wasn't all Tony wanted to do. He couldn't go home without stopping these men from hurting anyone else. He pulled rubble down from the caves, smashing all of their weapons to pieces.

Upon returning home, Tony promised that he would never sell weapons to anyone again.

Not only that, he would put his genius to work creating something that would make the world better, smarter and safer!

Tony also kept working in secret to refine and redesign his Iron Man armour, so he could protect the world from the weapons he wouldn't be able to stop.

Tony kept upgrading his armour over the years to come. He fought tirelessly to keep the world safe.

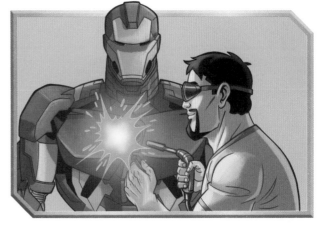

Eventually, he became a founding member of Earth's Mightiest Heroes, the Avengers!

Tony Stark wouldn't be remembered for his time creating weapons used for evil.

Instead, the world would come to know him for his red-and-gold armour. The world would call him a Super Hero.

He was Tony Stark, the Invincible Iron Man!

Time Warp Teamwork

One day, while the other Avengers were training, Tony Stark, a.k.a. Iron Man, was working on some new tech.

Sometimes, Tony felt very different from the other Avengers. They all had superhuman abilities.

Well, except for Black Widow and Hawkeye, but they didn't really count.

Their combat skills were way beyond what any normal human could do. All Tony had was his Iron Man suit.

When Tony got to the training room, the heroes were messing around.

Tony scratched his head. "What am I looking at here?"

"C'mon, Stark," said Hawkeye. "Lighten up. We're all just waiting for our next mission. There's no crime to stop right now."

So that's where you all fall short, thought Tony. *Time. I can fix that.*

Tony suited up for a test run and stepped onto the time machine.

"JARVIS," he commanded. "Set time for 2099, calculate crime ratios and synchronise the coordinates."

Over the next few days, Tony worked on combining specific elements of his Stark tech to create a powerful new tool.

Before long, Tony Stark had created a time machine.

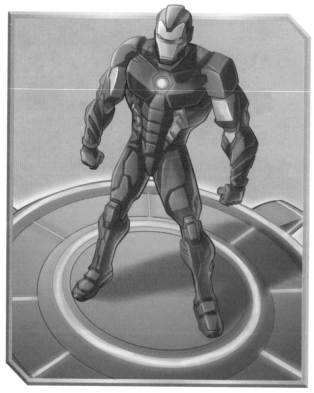

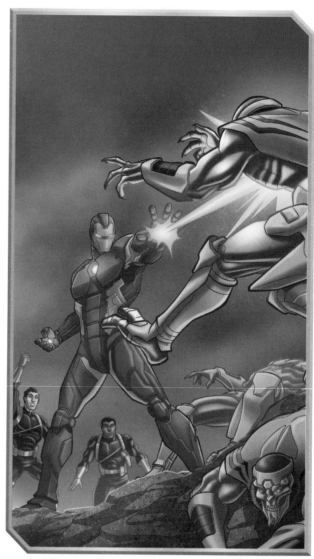

"Yes, sir," replied JARVIS.

Just like that, Iron Man was zapped to the year 2099 where the Chitauri were attacking a group of S.H.I.E.L.D. agents!

Iron Man sprang into action, swiftly taking down the Chitauri with blasts from his gauntlets. When they were defeated, Iron Man hit a button on his wrist. He was back in his lab a few moments later.

That afternoon, Iron Man called the Avengers into his lab to reveal his amazing new invention, but Captain America didn't think messing with time was a good idea.

Iron Man's temper flared. "No kidding, old man. I don't take being a Super Hero lightly… unlike some people."

Captain America's eyes narrowed. "How does everyone else feel about it? This is a democracy, after all."

The other Avengers thought fighting crime, in whatever time period, was a good idea.

"Here are your missions," said Iron Man.

"Black Widow and Hawkeye," announced JARVIS, "prepare to travel to 1840."

The pair were suddenly outside Buckingham Palace, where Queen Victoria was under attack! Using their stealth and speed, the heroes took down the attacker.

Then, with the push of a button, they were back in the lab.

Captain America, Hulk and Thor battled evil robot wolves in the year 4029.

"Ah-woooo!" howled Thor.

After defeating the robots, they zapped back to the lab.

destroy a local village.

Iron Man and the masked rider fired their weapons at each other and everything suddenly went pitch-black.

Iron Man opened his eyes. He was on the ground.

Soon, it was Iron Man's turn. The time machine rattled violently. Too violently. Iron Man arrived in the year 1792.

A masked man came round the corner, using his blasters to

Iron Man looked around. Then, he saw the villain ride round the corner again. So, Iron Man got up and they both fired their weapons... again.

The same thing kept happening again and again and again.

"I'm stuck in a time loop," said Iron Man, and he had no idea how to escape.

Back in the lab, the team realised Iron Man was in trouble.

They looked through Tony's plans, searching for a way to bring him back.

Finally, they came up with a plan. If it didn't work, Iron Man would be stuck forever.

Black Widow pointed her

gauntlets at the machine, destroying the circuitry. Suddenly, the portal opened onto the strange desert scene. Cap leapt into action.

"I'm coming, buddy!" cried the Super-Soldier.

Captain America jumped through the portal and protected Iron Man with his vibranium shield.

"Oomph!" the villain cried out in surprise, before falling off his horse.

The time loop had been broken!

As the portal started to close, Cap and Iron Man jumped through, along with the captured villain.

The time machine was completely broken. Iron Man decided not to try and fix it.

"You were right, Cap," he said. "Time travel isn't something to take lightly."

Cap put his arm round his friend. "Good advice. Even from an old man like me."

Blue Steel

If there was one thing Tony Stark loved, it was inventing new gadgets. "Just a few more tweaks," Tony muttered to himself, "and I will be— Oh, wait, what's this?"

An image of chaos and panic flashed across his screens. A train station in the city was under attack by an unknown enemy!

"Guess this will have to wait until later," said Tony, rushing to put on his Iron Man armour. When he first made the suit, it took forever to put on.

Now, the individual pieces of armour automatically flew to his body as he hurried to save the day.

"Come on, helmet, don't be late," said Tony.

On the other side of town, men and women scattered in fear as one of the trains lurched and careened off its track, coming close to slamming into some passengers.

Iron Man arrived just in time to pluck a commuter out of the way. Then he saw the villain who was causing all the locomotion commotion.

Iron Man's eyes narrowed as he confronted the villain. It was someone Iron Man recognised. "I didn't realise there was a Cyclone in today's weather forecast."

"Not just any Cyclone," the villain replied. "I'm a Category Five!"

He whipped up a funnel of wind and launched a train carriage towards the Super Hero.

Acting quickly, Iron Man flew up and intercepted the train carriage before it smashed into the crowd of innocent commuters. Then, he guided it back down to the track.

"Category Five, huh?" said Iron Man. "Wouldn't have anything to do with those jet thrusters on your back, would it?"

"Are you jealous?" taunted Cyclone.

"Say, did you ask the salesman if your jets can handle an electromagnetic pulse?" cried Iron Man over the wind.

"A what?" replied Cyclone.

"Never mind, let's just test it out," said Iron Man, activating an electromagnetic pulse in his own armour. The magnetic waves quickly fanned out and promptly disabled the thrusters in Cyclone's jetpack.

"Whoaaaa!" cried Cyclone, as he sputtered and spun out of control. Iron Man knocked the villain out cold just as the wind finally died down.

"Of those hunks of junk? Think again," replied Iron Man. "Besides, I bet I can still out-fly you any day."

The villain smirked as his jetpack began to whir even louder and the winds grew even stronger. "We'll see about that!"

Iron Man knew he needed to disable Cyclone's jetpack before the villain created a full-blown hurricane.

Back in his lab, Tony Stark had time to examine Cyclone's jetpack more closely.

"This is pretty intense technology," noted Tony. "How did Cyclone get his hands on something like this?"

As he continued to tinker, Tony suddenly realised where he recognised the technology from: "This has to be the work of A.I.M. scientists!"

A.I.M. – or Advanced Idea Mechanics – was a group of brilliant, evil scientists whose goal was to use technology to create disorder and chaos. If they were selling weapons and technology to the likes of Cyclone, that could only mean trouble.

"I've got to stop them," said Tony, "and I think I know how. If those A.I.M. goons think it's funny to give Cyclone all that extra horsepower, how about I give them a taste of their own medicine?"

Tony put on his Iron Man suit and took off for the A.I.M. research facility with his new invention. "Time to throw a wrench in their operation. Come on, let's go… Blue Crew? Blue Dude? Uhh, we'll figure it out later."

The A.I.M. research facility was well guarded, but Iron Man had a plan.

Tony activated one of his autonomous battle robots and mounted Cyclone's jetpack onto its back. Then he installed a propeller on the base so that it would create a small whirlwind as it flew, just like Cyclone!

One of the guards spotted him. "Look! It's Iron Man and... what is that?!" he cried.

"Hello, boys," said Iron Man, confidently. "How's the weather down there?"

Suddenly, both Iron Man and his new invention blasted the guards. Not only had he given his new invention Cyclone's jetpack, he had also given him super-powered water guns!

Caught by surprise, the A.I.M. guards didn't have time to defend themselves, and the facility began to flood. Iron Man smiled. "What, you guys don't like water slides?"

Iron Man's plan had worked!

"See, this is what happens when you sell dangerous technology to people," said Iron Man. "Like karma, it always comes back around."

"You won't get away with this, Iron Man," the A.I.M. leader said bitterly.

"Actually, I already have," replied Iron Man. "Oh, and by the way, I'm keeping the jetpack. I need Blue Steel for my next pool party."

Captain America
Steve Rogers

Are you ready to travel back in time? Good! Because we're headed back to the 1940s, when the world was at war! This is where we meet Captain America. But before he was Captain America, he was Steve Rogers!

- Height: 6' 2"
- Occupation: Avenger
- Recipient of the Super-Soldier serum
- The pinnacle of human physical potential
- Heightened strength, endurance and agility
- Master hand-to-hand fighter
- Skilled military leader and strategist with a strong sense of honour and justice
- Equipped with a virtually indestructible vibranium shield

As war broke out across the world in the 1940s, ruthless forces like Hydra, directed by the villainous Red Skull, Arnim Zola and Baron Zemo tore through Europe. The world was in need of a hero, someone to stand up and fight for all people, and no one would ever have guessed who that hero would turn out to be.

In the borough of Brooklyn in the great city of New York, a young boy named Steve Rogers sat, dismayed by the newsreels he would see each week in his local theatre. War was engulfing the world, and it seemed like no one could stop it.

Steve watched as evil swarmed. Though he was small and suffered from asthma, he wanted desperately to help fight for what was right. But the army only saw Steve's size, and wouldn't let him join.

But Steve never gave up. So, on his seventeenth attempt to enlist in the army, he was finally let in!

He was surprised to hear that he'd be part of a secret operation called 'Project: Rebirth'.

tests, only one of them would receive the treatment to become a Super-Soldier. Doctor Erskine finally chose Steve Rogers for the experiment.

The scientists, led by Doctor Erskine, wanted to create a Super-Soldier!

Though all the candidates were put through intense physical training, as well as other

It was more important to Erskine to find someone who cared about right and wrong, and the American spirit, than to find someone with muscles.

Steve drank Erskine's secret formula, was encased in a metal box and then bombarded with Vita Rays. Anyone else would have been scared, but all Steve could think about was finally getting a chance to help those in need.

Within seconds, the transformation was complete: where once stood a 44-kilogram weakling, now stood the world's first and only Super-Soldier!

Steve wasted no time getting straight to work, fighting for freedom across the globe!

Nicknamed Captain America by both the army and press, Steve helped turn the tide of the war and beat back the evil forces running wild!

But even Captain America couldn't save the world alone. Along with the brave soldiers of the world's finest armies, Captain America met other heroes, including his sidekick Bucky Barnes. The two became best friends during the war, although their friendship would last far longer than either of them could ever have imagined.

Zemo's castle was loaded with deadly defences, but by working together, Steve and Bucky overcame them. Just as they grabbed the fiend, Zemo launched a powerful rocket towards New York City. Steve's home was in danger!

Near the end of the war, Captain America and Bucky tracked Baron Zemo to his family castle. Steve wanted to stop the villain once and for all.

But Zemo would not be stopped so easily!

Thinking fast, Steve jumped onto the rocket, taking him far into the sky, and out to sea. He broke the rocket's wings just in time, causing it to fall harmlessly into the freezing ocean below!

remain in the icy depths until he was found, many years later, by a group of heroes like him, a group inspired by him, none other than the Avengers.

While Captain America would have countless adventures as part of the Avengers, one thing never changed. Behind Captain America's shield, Steve Rogers would always remain just a kid from Brooklyn who always wanted to do the right thing.

But the victory came at a price; Steve had fallen into the cold waters as well! He would

Thor
Prince of Asgard

Thor is a prince from the realm of Asgard, whose father is named Odin. Thor also wields a mystic hammer named Mjolnir. But Thor wasn't always worthy...

- Height: 6' 6"
- Occupation: Prince of Asgard
- Son of Odin
- Superhuman strength, speed, endurance and resistance to injury
- Virtually immortal
- His enchanted hammer, Mjolnir, grants mastery over the elements of thunder and lightning
- Can fly and open interdimensional gateways using Mjolnir
- Raised alongside his brother, Loki the Trickster

The Asgardian Prince

The Mighty Thor was once the most powerful being in the magical realm of Asgard. The only way to reach this world was by a bridge called the Bifrost. Even though Asgard and the people who lived there were well protected, they faced endless threats.

Thor was one of the land's great protectors.

Thor was born the son of Odin, Lord of Asgard, making Thor a prince. Thor and his brother, Loki, the adopted son of Odin, lived in a grand palace. As children, Thor and Loki each wanted to prove their worth to their father. Eventually, Loki grew jealous of Thor because he was the favoured son. The throne was Thor's by right.

To determine when Thor would be ready to rule, Odin had a special hammer made. It was forged from a mystical metal taken from the heart of a dying star. It held great power, but only someone who proved to be worthy could lift the hammer, Mjolnir!

Thor performed amazing acts of bravery and nobility, all while displaying great strength.

With every great achievement, Thor would try to pick up Mjolnir. One day, when it seemed he would never be able to raise the hammer, Thor grasped it, and lifted it high up into the air. He had proven himself worthy of his weapon, and he used it well.

Thor was cursed by his father to live on Earth as a mere mortal!

Odin made his son believe that he was Don Blake, a medical student who had an injured leg. As Don, Thor learned to study hard, and eventually he earned his medical degree.

Odin wanted Thor to be a great warrior, and he had become one. More importantly, Odin knew Thor had earned every Asgardian's respect. But Odin also knew that Thor had begun to let the power go to his head. Odin was not happy.

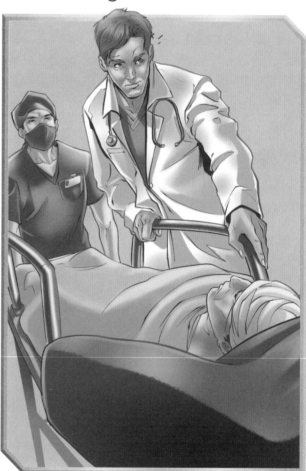

He allowed others to help him with his injury. In doing so, he learned to truly love humanity.

Then, one day, on holiday in Norway, Don discovered a strange walking stick inside a cave.

When he struck the stick against the ground it magically transformed.

It was Mjolnir in disguise!

Odin was pleased. His son had learnt humility. He had become human in spirit, but still, now and forever, he was the Mighty Thor.

On Earth, Loki coerced the Incredible Hulk into fits of rage in order to draw Thor into battle. When Thor realised that the Hulk had been manipulated by Loki, he knew he was going to need some help.

As he fought super villains all over the world, Thor's presence attracted the attention of his brother, Loki, who had embraced his mischievous and devious side while his brother had been away.

Loki had just the plan for defeating his pesky older brother.

With the assistance of Iron Man, Ant-Man and Wasp, the heroes defeated Loki and forced him to confess his crimes. Thor knew he needed to continue to protect the people of earth and Asgard from evil, and he couldn't do it alone.

From that moment on, Thor was part of the Avengers, the greatest team of heroes the universe has ever witnessed!

Doom of Fin Fang Foom

A bolt of lightning cracked across the sky as Thor landed on top of Avengers Tower. He had just defeated the Enchantress, and was looking forward to regaling his fellow Avengers with stories of his epic triumph.

"Hulk! Captain America!" boomed Thor, as he walked into the training room. "Come hear about my latest conquest."

Captain America and Hulk rolled their eyes. Being friends with Thor was great, but the guy could be really big-headed sometimes.

"Hulk, come here and let me show you how I did it," said Thor. Hulk reluctantly walked over. "There's my colossal comrade!"

Suddenly, Thor used his hammer to put Hulk in a headlock. "So, see what I'm doing here?" said Thor encouragingly. "Cap! Are you watching?"

"Look buddy," began Captain America, "don't be so rough with Hulk. He may be a green Goliath, but he's still your friend."

"Hulk annoyed," said Hulk. Thor wasn't really listening to what Captain America was saying. He didn't think he was being too rough with Hulk.

"You come back from these battles with a pretty big head," continued Cap. "Just be careful, or one day you may find yourself in a major fight without any backup."

Thor shrugged his shoulders and headed straight to the lab to look for Nick Fury. As Thor waited, he glanced at one of the glowing screens. Lazily, he touched it, and it suddenly slid down to reveal a tiny dragon! Thor examined the strange object. *Huh. Weird,* he thought, as he set the figurine onto the table.

With nothing else to do, Thor began to daydream. He thought back to his fight with the Enchantress and began to re-enact the battle.

Thor swung his hammer dramatically in the air. "Nice try, Enchantress! Bow before Thor, son of—"

Suddenly, he heard a tiny crack. Thor had accidentally knocked over the dragon, breaking it in half! The room quickly began to fill with thick, green smoke.

As the smoke cleared, it revealed a massive hole in the side of the tower! But it wasn't the hole that was worrying Thor, it was the forty-four-foot dragon monster that had just materialised!

"Who has awoken Fin Fang Foom from his slumber?" the monster bellowed, his voice shaking the windows of Avengers Tower.

"Prepare to be defeated, beast!" said Thor, raising his hammer above his head.

"You dare challenge me?" replied Fin Fang Foom, laughing. "I have wreaked havoc upon this planet before, and I will do it again. Over and over. Humanity will pay for the crimes they've committed against my kind!"

Fin Fang Foom smashed his massive hand against the crumbling wall of Avengers Tower. The entire building shook from the impact, throwing Thor off-balance. He steadied himself and attacked Fin Fang Foom with his mighty hammer. But the monster didn't even flinch.

"Ha-ha-ha! Nice try, puny warrior," said Fin Fang Foom.

Hearing the commotion, Hulk and Captain America rushed into the lab. When they saw the monster, their mouths fell open.

Cap began to shout orders. "Hulk! Ready on my—!"

But Fin Fang Foom landed one final blow to Thor, then turned to smile at the heroes.

"Well, I better be off. Things to do, places to see… and destroy!"

With that, he flew away.

Thor looked back at his friends, his eyes dark with anger. "Don't follow me."

Hulk looked at Cap. "Must help Thor."

"I know, buddy," replied Captain America. "He's too proud to ask for our help, but we're a team and we always look out for our friends when they're in need."

Hulk watched Cap pick something up from off the floor.

"Cap have plan?" asked Hulk.

"I sure do, buddy," said Cap. "Let's go! We need to get to the Quinjet before it's too late."

The heroes quickly settled into the cockpit as Cap described his idea. "We need to get up in the air. We're looking for a giant dragon monster and an Asgardian warrior. How hard can it be to spot them?"

Meanwhile, Thor was on a mission of his own. He needed to defeat Fin Fang Foom himself. After all, he broke the tiny dragon figurine.

How could I have been so careless? thought Thor. *I am an Avenger. The safety of this planet is my responsibility.*

As Thor flew through the air, he could see Fin Fang Foom soaring above some skyscrapers. Thor watched as the monstrous beast landed on top of a massive unfinished building. It was exactly where Thor wanted him.

Thor knew if he could knock out the monster, it would buy him some time to figure out how to send him back to where he came from. Thor dived straight for the powerful beast. Then, with one mighty lunge, he used his hammer to hit the beast right in the gut!

"You are like a child with your silly attempts at defeating me!" roared Fin Fang Foom. As if he were batting away a pesky fly,

Fin Fang Foom smacked Thor with his giant hand. Thor went crashing to the ground, along with half the building!

"There," grunted Hulk, pointing to the growing cloud of smoke. The heroes landed the Quinjet and ran over to Thor. He wasn't moving, but soon they were able to rouse him.

"Brothers, I am—" began Thor, but Hulk cut him off.

"Save world now. Sorry later."

They were going to defeat this menace once and for all. Together.

Suddenly, they saw Fin Fang Foom dart past. He was headed straight for the Brooklyn Bridge!

Captain America, Hulk and Thor charged Fin Fang Foom as one mighty team.

The monster roared as he latched onto the bridge, rocking it back and forth. "You will regret the day you ever messed with the great, the powerful... Fin Fang Foom!"

Thor had an idea. "We must entrap the monster! Hulk, do what you do best!"

"Hulk smash!" cried Hulk, as he pummelled the beast, sending Fin Fang Foom crashing into the water below the bridge.

All seemed quiet, until the heroes heard a deep laugh from below. "Ha-ha-ha! You think a little water can trap me?"

"No, but this might," said Cap, as he produced the pieces Hulk saw him pick up off the floor back at Avengers Tower.

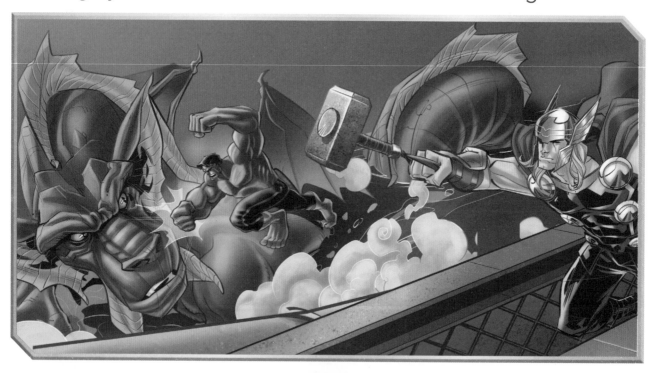

It was the broken dragon figurine.

When he brought the two pieces together, the monster screamed in pain.

"No!" Fin Fang Foom cried as he disappeared into a cloud of thick, green smoke. He was absorbed back into the figurine, repairing it completely. The monster was back where he belonged.

Thor turned to his friends. "Fellow warriors, I apologise for my arrogance. I should have listened."

"You're an Avenger," said Cap, after he put the tiny dragon safely into his pack. "We're family. But sometimes family can be annoying. Like, very annoying. Extremely—"

"Okay! I get it," said Thor.

"Back to training room?" asked Hulk. "Hulk bet he can smash puny Thor."

Thor smiled.

Black Panther
T'Challa

Did you know that one of the Avengers is an honest-to-goodness king? T'Challa, king of the African nation of Wakanda. You might know him better by another name: Black Panther!

- Height: 6' 0"
- Occupation: King of Wakanda
- Earned and inherited the title of Black Panther, protector of his people
- Heightened strength, speed, stamina, agility and reflexes
- Master of martial arts, acrobatics and handheld weaponry
- Utilises highly advanced Wakandan technology, including vibranium-woven body armour and stealth aircraft
- Genius-level intellect with expertise in physics and technology

The Legend of the Black Panther

Many years ago, an asteroid containing massive amounts of vibranium metal smashed into the Wakandan forest. Its unique ability to absorb vibrations made it valuable.

The land of Wakanda lay deep in the heart of Africa. A country born of great tribal traditions, it owed much of its majestic beauty to the thriving animal kingdom that roams its lands.

Thieves and warriors would invade Wakanda, looking to steal the vibranium. To keep the Wakandan people safe, their protector and king, the Black Panther, closed Wakanda's borders to outsiders.

T'Chaka had a son named T'Challa. He and his wife, Ramonda, taught the young prince everything they could. T'Chaka asked a lot of his son. T'Challa felt that he was never good enough for his father, but knew that one day he was supposed to take over as king, and as Black Panther.

Years passed, and the current Wakandan king and Black Panther was T'Chaka.

He was worthy of the mantle of Black Panther through hard work, study and training.

Instead of giving up, T'Challa decided he would be the best at everything he did.

He learnt more and trained harder, desperately trying to live up to his father's expectations.

When he grew older, T'Challa asked his father if he could take the trials of the Black Panther.

right hand, Klaw projected a stampede of animals made of sound. The animals infiltrated the land of Wakanda and quickly overpowered its military forces.

As Black Panther, T'Chaka took to Wakanda's defence. He did not know that his son, T'Challa, would often leave the palace and follow him.

But T'Chaka told his son that he was not ready yet.

Soon after, Wakanda was attacked by an outsider named Klaw, a man who was pure sonic energy.

Klaw wanted Wakanda's vibranium. Using a sonic converter he wore over his

T'Challa would watch, proud, as his father defeated any foe who dared to challenge the kingdom.

This time was different, though. Klaw had seized the vibranium and was getting away.

T'Chaka was not about to allow Klaw to steal from Wakanda. He arrived just as the villain was making his escape.

T'Challa jumped to action. He grabbed a vibranium disc and used it to shield himself from Klaw's powers as he advanced.

T'Chaka leapt at Klaw. The villain turned, unleashing his full power on T'Chaka. The king was badly wounded by the sudden blast.

Klaw wasn't able to blast T'Challa. The young boy moved quickly to press his advantage, using the vibranium disc to absorb all of the vibrations that Klaw let loose. When he was close enough, T'Challa raised the metal disc and brought it down on Klaw's arm, smashing the sonic converter!

Klaw was injured, but managed to escape as T'Challa rushed to his father's side. The young man held his dying father in his arms, vowing that he would become worthy to be called both king and Black Panther, and continue his father's legacy.

T'Challa became King of Wakanda and passed the Black Panther trials. He donned the costume and spent many years travelling in search of Klaw, to avenge his father.

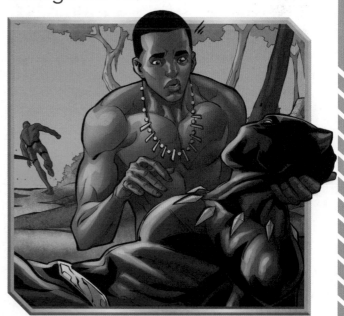

Those journeys took him on many adventures, and even led him to the Avengers, the legendary Super Hero team!

But as much as he was an Avenger, T'Challa was King of Wakanda and the Black Panther first and foremost.

The sweeping lands of his forefathers would always be first in T'Challa's heart.

Wakanda forever!

Klaw's Revenge

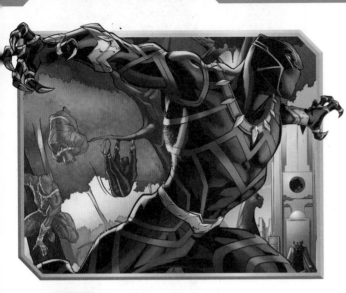

WHOOSH!

Black Panther leapt out of the Quinjet and swiftly caught hold of a jungle branch. He was returning home to the African kingdom of Wakanda after fighting crime with the Avengers.

As much as he enjoyed working with a team, T'Challa was happiest when he was home. He was still settling into his role as king and Black Panther. He had vowed to honour his father's legacy, but trying to live up to his greatness was taking a toll.

It was a difficult job, but T'Challa was determined to serve his country like his father before him.

A Black Panther's work is never done! thought T'Challa.

When T'Challa arrived home, he found his stepmother, Ramonda, waiting for him. "Welcome home, my son," she said, wrapping him in a big hug.

But T'Challa was tense. Ramonda could tell something was on his mind.

Suddenly, Okoye and Nakia, two of the Dora Milaje, warrior women sworn to protect the Wakandan king, burst into the room. There was an emergency.

T'Challa and Ramonda quickly followed the Dora Milaje to the council room.

There they found the tribal elders gathered around a large monitor. Everyone spoke in hushed tones as T'Challa approached.

"These energy readings are off the charts," said T'Challa, as he assessed the situation.

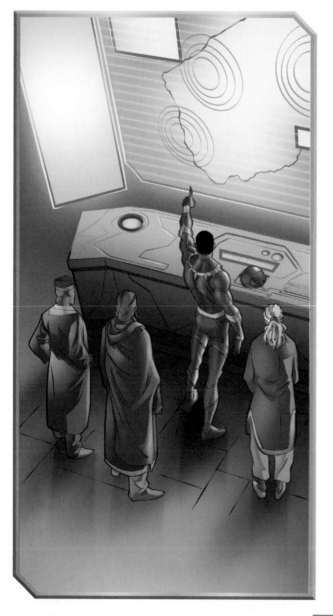

"There's only one person who could be behind this," said T'Challa. "Klaw."

Klaw was Wakanda's greatest enemy and the only outsider ever to infiltrate its walls.

The last time Klaw was in Wakanda, he had defeated T'Challa's father.

"Okoye. Nakia. Come with me," said T'Challa, banishing painful memories. "We need to stop Klaw before he reaches the palace!"

Meanwhile, Klaw was blasting his way underground using his sonic-powered arm. It was only a matter of time before he made it to the palace. Klaw had one thing on his mind. Revenge.

Little did Klaw know, Black Panther had been preparing for his return. The hero told Nakia and Okoye to go to his lab, grab the metal sphere on his desk and be ready for his signal.

Then, Black Panther led giant lorries loaded with long vibranium rods out of the city. "This way, towards the energy spikes!" commanded Black Panther.

They would cut Klaw off on his way into Wakanda.

"Quickly! Get into your positions!" shouted Black Panther.

The vibranium's sound-absorbing properties had the power to destroy Klaw's sonic form. It was the only thing that could stop his underground charge to the palace.

"Now!" cried Black Panther.

The trucks plunged the vibranium rods straight into the earth.

BOOM!

Klaw ran into the vibranium rods underground and jolted back violently. As he flew up from the dirt, Klaw cried out in pain. "Aaarrgh!"

Black Panther leapt off the truck and approached the motionless Klaw. Suddenly, the villain sprang to his feet.

The two enemies squared off: Black Panther versus Klaw, the ultimate showdown.

"Hello, old friend," taunted Klaw. "I was actually heading to the palace to see you. But I guess this place is as good as any to finally destroy the heir to the Wakandan throne."

"Funny," replied Black Panther. "I don't plan on giving up my throne anytime soon."

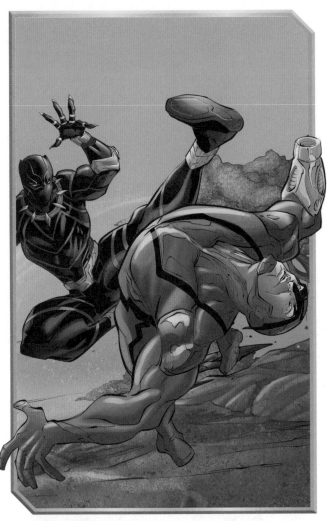

"Ha-ha-ha!" laughed Klaw, the sound echoing through the valley.

He approached Black Panther, who lay on his back, groaning in pain.

"Silly child. When you destroyed my arm all those years ago, I vowed to take my revenge on the nation of Wakanda. And your end shall be my final act."

BOOMPH!

With a mighty kick, Black Panther sent Klaw flying through the air. Klaw didn't stand a chance. Well, at least that's what Black Panther thought.

But Klaw had a powerful sonic arm. It could send blasts of pure sound to stun his enemies.

Klaw drew back his arm as it began to whir with power. The villain launched a thunderous blast towards Black Panther, slamming the hero into the ground.

Like a flash of lightning, Black Panther's legs smashed into the villain.

"You talk too much," growled Black Panther, as he watched Klaw's body soar through the air. It was exactly what Black Panther had planned. "Nakia. Okoye. The sphere!"

The Dora Milaje warriors had been hiding in the brush, waiting for Black Panther's signal. Okoye's eyes narrowed. "Don't mess with Wakanda!" she cried.

She tossed the small grey sphere on to the ground. It expanded like a balloon to envelop Klaw. He was trapped inside.

Klaw cried out from his see-through prison. "What... what is this? What's happening?"

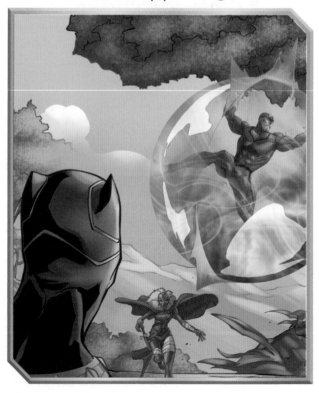

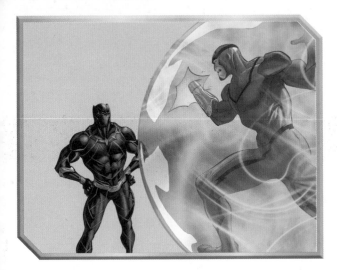

Black Panther placed his hands on his hips proudly. "It's my latest invention," he said. "A spherical prison made entirely of vibranium. I knew you'd be back, Klaw. I came prepared."

With Klaw locked away, Black Panther gathered his people in the city square.

"Our nation has faced many threats over the years," he said. "Although I cannot promise the threats will end, I do promise to protect you like my father before me. I shall continue his legacy, not only as king, but as Black Panther."

The people of Wakanda cheered, proud to have someone as brave and honourable as T'Challa for their king and protector.

Okoye
Leader of the Dora Milaje

Okoye serves with distinction as head of the Dora Milaje – warrior women tasked with protecting the leader of Wakanda. Okoye places her duty to Wakanda above all else. With her fierce and noble spirit, Okoye is prepared to make any sacrifice to keep her people safe and free.

- Height: 5' 9"
- Occupation: Dora Milaje warrior
- One of T'Challa's top advisors
- Fierce and noble spirit
- Master of hand-to-hand combat

Vibranium Conundrum

"**W**akanda forever!" T'Challa saluted the Dora Milaje as he exited his ship.

"Welcome home," said his younger sister, Princess Shuri. "How was the United Nations meeting?"

"I always enjoy meeting with the other world leaders," said T'Challa. "But let's just say it is good to be back home."

"It is good you're back," replied Shuri. "There is trouble at the border."

T'Challa and Shuri joined Okoye and a group of Wakandan farmers in the palace throne room.

One by one, the farmers pulled up pictures of their land.

Sheep had gone missing, crops had been wiped out and construction vehicles had been destroyed!

"Help us, my king," the final farmer pleaded. "Whoever, or whatever, has infiltrated our border is destroying our land and our livelihood."

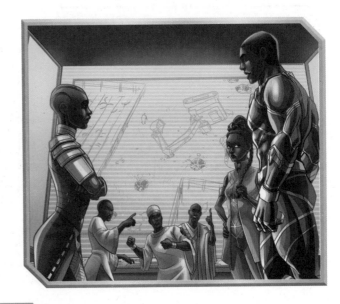

"If the border has been breached we must find the culprit at once," urged T'Challa. "Okoye and I will investigate."

"I'm coming, too!" insisted Princess Shuri.

"This is just a recon mission, Shuri," explained T'Challa. "To see what the threat might be."

Shuri smiled. "Exactly. If we find that the threat is out there, we need to protect what remains immediately." She lifted her hand and held up a high-tech ring. "What better protection than the portable vibranium shield I invented?"

The trio headed out to the farmland. "These tracks look fresh," said Black Panther, studying the ground.

"And the sheep are frightened," added Shuri. "We can't just leave them here."

Black Panther thought for a moment, then turned to Shuri. "We will take them with us." He pointed to her ring. "Under your vibranium shield."

Black Panther and Okoye followed the tracks from the farm and into the forest.

They soon came upon the missing sheep. They were hiding from someone, or something.

"You're safe now," said Black Panther, directing each sheep on the path back towards the shield.

Soon, they heard a faint noise ahead – a deep, throaty grunting.

They quickly hid.

Suddenly, one of the branches cracked and a creature appeared through the large leaves. It turned its head and locked eyes on Black Panther and Okoye, letting out a ferocious roar!

"It's a giant wild boar!" said Okoye. "And it looks like we just interrupted his lunch, come on!"

Black Panther and Okoye chased after the boar as it darted past them.

Black Panther saw that the boar was heading straight for where Shuri and the sheep were standing, her vibranium shield covering them.

"Shuri, watch out!" cried Black Panther.

Shuri held firm, and so did the shield.

"Mission accomplished," she said, proudly. "Now what?"

"We need to immobilise it!" cried Okoye.

"I have an idea," said Black Panther, looking back towards the farm and its construction site. "Okoye," he began, "you're a fast runner, right?"

Okoye grinned, understanding what Black Panther had in mind. "Just try to keep up," she said.

The duo took off at full steam, leading the boar towards the farm.

"Now!" shouted Black Panther.

All at once, the two warriors stopped running and held their ground. The boar continued charging.

Just when it was nearly upon them, the duo leapt skilfully out of the way and the boar fell into a gigantic hole.

"Ah, the art of simple distraction," said T'Challa, with a grin. "Not like your fancy technology, Sister, but it did the job, eh?"

Shuri rolled her eyes. "Lucky break," she muttered. Then she clicked a button on her ring to deactivate the shield, but nothing happened. "Uh-oh," she said. "It's stuck!"

"Stand back!" cried T'Challa, getting a running start.

He hurled a flying kick at the shield, but it didn't budge. "Sister, how do we pull the plug on this thing?"

Shuri's eyes lit up. "I know! The vibranium is programmed to defend against attacks, but if you approach it slowly, it should recognise the tech in your suit and pair up."

Black Panther raised his hand slowly and rested it against the shield. "It's working, I can control it now!"

T'Challa soon freed his sister and the sheep from inside the shield.

"I guess my tech still needs some work," said Shuri, after she and the sheep had been freed.

"Princess," said Okoye, kindly. "Your technology is wonderful. But sometimes it takes machines and human beings working together to be successful."

"You're right," replied Shuri, nodding. Then, poking T'Challa, she said, "I guess I will let you figure out how to get that boar back to where it belongs!"

Shuri
Wakandan Scientist and Princess

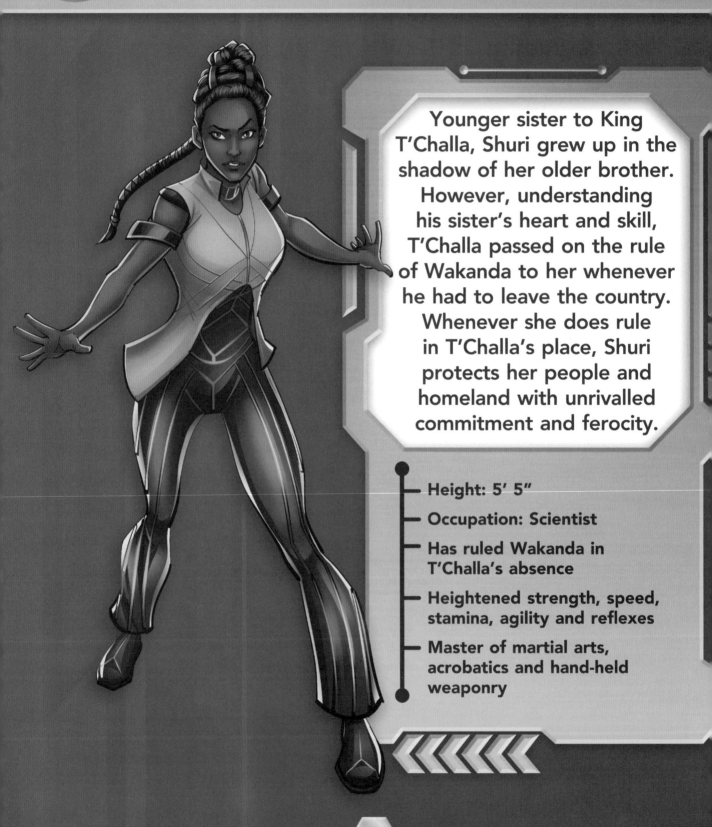

Younger sister to King T'Challa, Shuri grew up in the shadow of her older brother. However, understanding his sister's heart and skill, T'Challa passed on the rule of Wakanda to her whenever he had to leave the country. Whenever she does rule in T'Challa's place, Shuri protects her people and homeland with unrivalled commitment and ferocity.

- Height: 5' 5"
- Occupation: Scientist
- Has ruled Wakanda in T'Challa's absence
- Heightened strength, speed, stamina, agility and reflexes
- Master of martial arts, acrobatics and hand-held weaponry

CRRAACK!
A massive sound jolted through Avengers Tower, where Shuri and T'Challa were showing Doctor Bruce Banner some Wakandan tech.

"I'll explain later!" cried Captain Marvel.

Black Panther raced to help, while Shuri ran back to the lab to grab her gauntlets. Banner turned into the Hulk and followed T'Challa into the fight.

To find out what the noise was, the heroes rushed to the roof, where they saw Captain Marvel fighting Proxima Midnight! She was one of Thanos's strongest allies.

"What's she doing here?" asked Shuri.

Captain Marvel flew back to the roof, where the other Avengers were waiting.

"Two members of the Black Order have come to Earth – Proxima Midnight and Corvus Glaive," said Captain Marvel.

Realising she was outnumbered, Proxima Midnight opened up a portal.

"No, wait!" cried Captain Marvel. She needed to know what Proxima Midnight was doing on Earth.

But before Captain Marvel could reach her, the villain disappeared!

"Corvus got away while I was chasing Proxima," she continued. "I don't know where he is now."

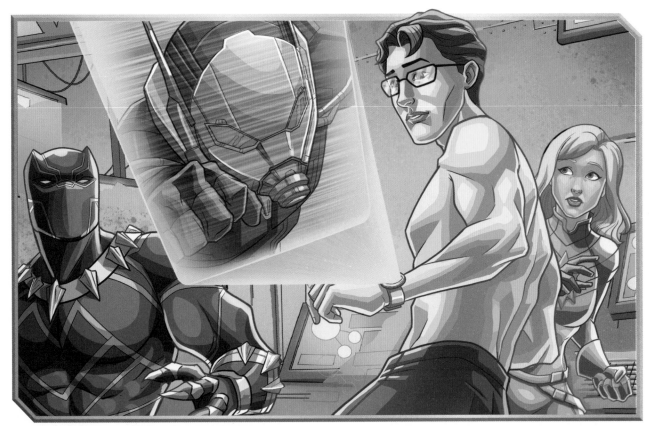

Suddenly, Banner got a distress call from Ant-Man. The small Super Hero's face filled the screen.

"Banner, help!" cried Ant-Man.

A golden blade swiped past the tiny hero as the others watched on.

"That's Corvus Glaive's weapon," said Captain Marvel, urgently.

"Look," said Banner, pointing at the map. "We have to get to the waterfront!"

"I'll catch up!" called Shuri from the lab. Her gauntlets weren't working properly and she had to fix them.

"Hurry, Sister!" cried Black Panther, who knew Shuri's gauntlets would be essential.

"I can answer that," replied Corvus Glaive. "Thanos wants Ant-Man because he wants to know how Pym Particles work."

Pym Particles were responsible for giving Ant-Man his powers to grow and shrink. In the hands of Thanos, the particles would be turned into a super-weapon!

The heroes soon arrived at the waterfront.

"Boy, am I glad to see you guys!" said Ant-Man. "Who is this guy?"

Captain Marvel blasted the villain with an energy beam, and said, "Corvus Glaive. One of Thanos's friends. What I don't know is why he's after you."

Corvus Glaive had to be stopped!

Though he was a tough opponent, Corvus Glaive struggled against four Super Heroes.

BAM!

Black Panther landed a surprise kick, bringing the villain to his knees, at which point Captain Marvel discharged an energy blast.

Corvus Glaive was still standing, but barely.

"I think we got him beat!" cried Ant-Man. "No Pym Particles for you, pal!"

But just as Hulk was about to deliver the final blow Proxima Midnight reappeared!

"You were barely able to handle one of us," gloated Proxima Midnight. "How can you fight us both?"

"I was wondering that myself," said Ant-Man, as the rest of his friends gathered to protect him.

Without the whole team in place, the heroes had their hands full!

Any moment, she would teleport away with him, and Thanos would have the secret of Pym Particles and the key to controlling the galaxy. How could the heroes stop them? *POW!*

Corvus smashed Black Panther into Captain Marvel.

"I feel like we could really use Shuri and those new-and-improved blasters right about now," said Captain Marvel.

"Um… guys? Over here?" Ant-Man gave a nervous chuckle as he struggled against Proxima Midnight.

Shuri appeared out of nowhere and knocked Proxima Midnight flying with an energy punch from her mended gauntlets.

Ant-Man was set free!

"She hits like the Hulk!" cried Captain Marvel, happily.

With Shuri's tech, the Super Heroes quickly gained the upper hand.

"Better late than never!" Black Panther called out to his sister.

Shuri laughed. "The combination of Wakandan and Stark tech is unbeatable!"

"Abort mission!" cried Proxima Midnight.

Before the heroes could grab them, the villains disappeared through a portal.

"Whew," said Ant-Man. "That was close."

"Piece of cake," said Shuri. "All we had to do was work together."

Hulk
Bruce Banner

Scientists don't come much smarter than Bruce Banner! He was an expert on gamma rays. In fact, his work with gamma rays eventually led him to become the Hulk!

- Height: 5' 9" as Bruce / 8' 5" as Hulk
- Occupation: Nuclear physicist
- Exposed to a massive dose of Gamma Radiation
- Transforms from Bruce Banner to Hulk when made angry or anxious
- Incredible superhuman strength, durability and healing factor
- Becomes more powerful as his anger increases
- As Banner, possesses a genius-level intellect
- Misunderstood by those around him due to the damage he can cause

Unlike his body, Bruce's brain was very strong. He grew up reading everything he could about science, maths and chemistry. Bruce found teachers like Professor Crawford who believed in him and helped him become a scientist.

Bruce Banner wasn't always the Avenger known as the Hulk. Long ago, he was just a little boy in school, no different than many others. He was small for his age and was bullied by many of his larger classmates.

One day, Bruce made his most exciting discovery yet – he figured out how to use Gamma Radiation to cure the sick!

But General Ross had other plans for the Gamma Radiation.

General Ross ordered Bruce and Professor Crawford to stop using it to help the sick – instead, he wanted a gamma bomb to help the army in war!

Bruce didn't want to make a bomb, but Ross insisted. Bruce felt intimidated by Ross and was scared to say no. He was being bullied once again.

After months of work, the bomb was set up in a remote desert. The team was about to detonate the bomb as they watched from a concrete bunker.

Suddenly, a truck appeared and stopped next to the bomb test site! Bruce saw a young driver and shouted that someone had to rescue him before the bomb exploded!

But the countdown to detonation had already begun – the bomb was going to go off!

Bruce begged the army heroes who were at the site to try and save the driver. But the men just told him to go away.

Something stirred inside Bruce, a feeling he hadn't noticed before.

It was courage! It was an inner strength! Not muscle, but heart! Bruce was done being bullied.

Without another word, Bruce charged out into the bright desert!

Unaware of the danger, the young man had hopped out of his truck and jumped up on the bonnet, a harmonica in one hand.

The bomb was just seconds away from detonation when Bruce reached the young man. At the last moment, Bruce pushed him into the protective ditch close by just as the bomb went off!

But Bruce was caught in the gamma blast!

General Ross and the army came out to inspect the bomb site.

The smoke was thinning out, but there was no sign of Bruce or the boy. Only the melted truck was visible.

Just as they started to fear the worst, a giant shape appeared in the smoke, standing over the young man to protect him.

It was the *Incredible Hulk!*

The Hulk, thinking that the army might hurt the young driver, defended him, snatching up tanks and tossing them aside. The army seemed like bullies, and the Hulk didn't like bullies. Hulk wasn't trying to hurt anyone, he just wanted to keep the boy safe.

But the army seemed scared Hulk would hurt them, and so they ran away from him.

After Hulk was sure that the young driver was going to be okay, he flexed his powerful legs and jumped miles into the air, far away from everyone.

Once Hulk was alone in the woods, he shrank and turned back into Bruce Banner. The gamma bomb's energy had been soaked up by Banner's body like a sponge. It made him strong and powerful, just like he had always wanted! But it didn't make Bruce happy. He was afraid he'd lose control as the Hulk and turn into a bully himself.

So Bruce decided he would walk away from his life and friends, and travel in search of a cure for what he thought was a monster inside of him.

Bruce Banner's journey would take him on many great adventures, and even though he would never believe it himself, he – and Hulk – were great heroes with great courage and strength. One day, the Hulk would even be an Avenger!

Bruce couldn't understand why his cousin, Jennifer Walters, was defending the beast.

Ravage was an evil monster who had stolen Bruce's DNA to give himself superhuman powers. But Jennifer was determined to see that he got a fair trial.

Bruce Banner watched closely as Ravage's cage was wheeled into court. Ravage, once known as Professor Crawford, was standing trial for a number of violent crimes.

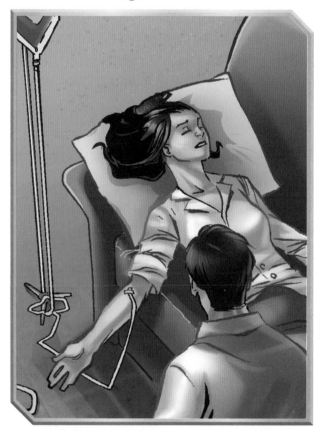

She knew what it was like to be seen as a monster. After all, she was She-Hulk, a mutant Super Hero created after Bruce had used his own DNA to save her life.

courtroom wall and jumped down into the city below.

But before Jennifer could speak, Ravage let out a terrible roar.

"Get out of my head!" he bellowed, as he ripped his way out of the cage.

"Order in the court!" cried the judge.

But Ravage took no notice. He smashed through the

"Time to get angry," said Bruce. His skin turned green and his muscles ripped through his shirt. He had transformed into Hulk.

He leapt out of the window and landed on the tarmac with a *THUD!*

Jennifer quickly changed into her She-Hulk costume and

chased after her cousin. But as she leapt through the city, she saw a mysterious woman following Hulk.

She-Hulk finally caught up with Hulk, and together they faced up to the strange woman.

"Hello, lovely creatures," she sang. "I am called Mercy. Come with me."

"No thanks," She-Hulk replied.

Mercy's sweet smile turned into a terrible grin. Then she unleashed a powerful blast that knocked both heroes to the ground.

Hulk staggered to his feet and charged at the villain. But Mercy stepped sideways, and Hulk ran straight into a brick wall.

"Lovely," purred Mercy. "Your anger feeds my power. The angrier you get the stronger I become. But listen. I want to help you. I can help you sleep for all eternity."

Suddenly, Hulk and She-Hulk realised what had happened to Ravage in court. His mind was under Mercy's control. They needed to find him, and fast.

"Back off, lady!" She-Hulk cried, leaping into action.

She grabbed Mercy and slammed her to the ground.

"Ouch!" wailed Mercy. "You may have defeated me, She-Hulk, but I still control the mind of your other friend. Ravage has so much anger. It's delicious."

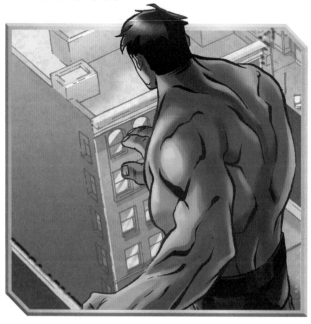

They didn't have to look far. Suddenly, *BOOM!* Ravage smashed into Hulk, and they both crashed to the ground. Hulk and Ravage roared with anger, shaking the windows of every building in the city.

As Hulk climbed out of the rubble, Ravage picked up a huge slab of concrete.

"Um, I don't think so!" yelled She-Hulk. She slammed into Ravage, knocking him to the ground. "Mercy still has him under her control. We need to knock some sense into him. Literally!"

She-Hulk drew back her fist and threw her most powerful punch.

Ravage was knocked out, breaking the connection with Mercy. Without his anger to feed on, the mysterious villain vanished.

Everyone held their breath as the judge read the sentencing. "I hereby find the defendant… not guilty."

Bruce cheered. Jennifer had done it!

As Bruce and Jennifer left the court, Bruce tried to cheer her up. "Don't worry," he said. "Ravage will be fine. He just needs to learn to control his anger, like I have."

Back in the courtroom, Ravage was put in a new, hi-tech cage.

Jennifer worked hard to convince the court that Ravage was not a monster. "He's an innocent man trapped in a monster's body," she told the men and women of the jury.

"I just wish there was more I could do," replied Jennifer.

Bruce smiled. "Just continue to fight for people like Ravage. Everybody could use a She-Hulk in their corner."

Black Widow
Natasha Romanoff

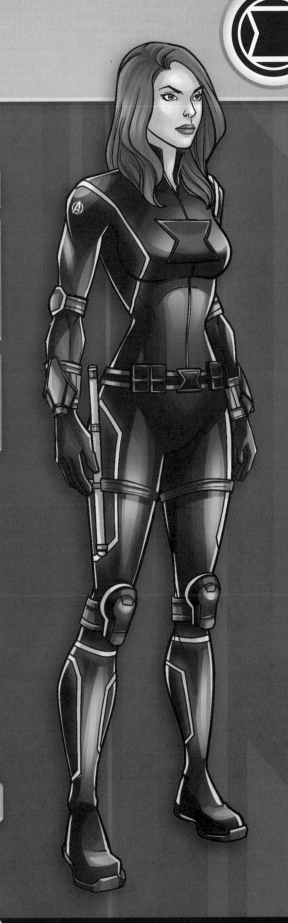

Everyone knows that a black widow spider is dangerous. And if you didn't know it, you do now, because we just told you. Anyway, meet Natasha Romanoff, aka Black Widow. She's every bit as dangerous as her namesake!

- Height: 5' 7"
- Occupation: Avenger
- Super-spy
- Master in the covert arts of espionage, infiltration and subterfuge
- Expert martial artist
- Exceptional agility and athletic ability
- Utilises advanced weaponry
- Trained from an early age in the top-secret Red Room programme

Natasha Romanoff, the Avenger known as Black Widow, was raised in Russia by a man named Ivan Petrovitch, who took Natasha under his wing when she was orphaned as a child.

Ivan trained Natasha in dance, acrobatics and gymnastics.

"Da, Natasha," said Ivan. "Good."

She was his best student.

Soon, word of Ivan's extraordinary student got around. One day, several government intelligence agents came and took young Natasha away from Ivan.

"Where are we going?" asked Natasha, more curious than frightened.

"Your destiny lies in the Black Widow programme," one of them answered.

Now Natasha was scared.

The agents brought Natasha to the Red Room. There, she would train to become a secret agent. She wasn't alone – other girls were training there, too.

The Red Room conditioned Natasha to serve the government above all else. It became her mother, father, sister and brother. She would defend it with her life, if needed.

In the Red Room, Natasha became a fierce fighter, a warrior with few equals. She trained in aikido, judo, karate and boxing.

After many years, Natasha earned the title of the Black Widow. Very few of the Red Room girls ever became Black Widows. It was a tremendous honour. Natasha was given a special uniform and two bracelets that fired 'widow's bite' bolts that could take down superhumans. With her new weapons and her flawless training, Natasha would be nearly unstoppable.

"I will not fail," vowed Natasha. She knew her duty. It was all she knew, all she was allowed to know.

Natasha ran many successful missions as a Black Widow.

She was always secret, always dangerous.

But once she was away from her trainers, Natasha began to see that what she was doing was wrong. People were getting hurt because of her.

She didn't like it… but she hadn't been shown any other way.

Natasha would occasionally encounter a hero called Hawkeye. Every time they met, she fought him with all her strength.

But there was something about him. Over time, his presence came to feel familiar, almost comforting. Eventually, they didn't even want to fight each other any more.

Instead, Natasha preferred just to talk to her new friend. He was one of the first people who had ever bothered to listen to her.

One day, Hawkeye said, "My name's Clint Barton. What's yours?"

"Why would you ask me that?" asked Black Widow, suspiciously.

"Because you're a person," replied Clint.

Black Widow didn't respond, but Hawkeye's question stuck with her. She'd been told for so long that her only purpose was as an agent, trained to serve.

"Yes," she said.

Natasha didn't know what would happen next. All she knew was that she was tired of serving the Red Room.

"I want to do good," she told Hawkeye. "I want to help people."

"I think I know just the person," replied Hawkeye.

Soon, they were both working for the trusted Director of S.H.I.E.L.D., Nick Fury.

Natasha didn't see Hawkeye for a while after that. But eventually, she was sent back to New York on a mission that could hurt many people.

She was hoping Hawkeye would find her… and he did.

"I don't want to do this any more," she told him, feeling hopeless.

"I can help you," said Hawkeye. "Will you trust me?"

Natasha looked at his open, honest face.

And then, one day, a threat descended upon Earth – Loki. "Black Widow, Hawkeye. I need you both," Nick Fury radioed over their comms. "This is going to take everything we've got. It's time to meet the others."

And suddenly, Natasha and Hawkeye were part of a team – a group of extraordinary people who had come together to defend Earth from super villains.

They were called the Avengers!

Natasha liked being part of a team. It was good to belong. But she never let herself forget the things she had done for the Red Room. She would always move faster, fight longer and work harder to be better.

After all, she had a past to make up for.

Nick Fury
Nicholas J. Fury

Nick Fury is the leader of an incredible organisation known as S.H.I.E.L.D., but what you don't know is that Nick Fury is the smartest, most dangerous spy on Earth!

- Height: 6' 3"
- Occupation: Director of S.H.I.E.L.D.
- Former U.S. Army sergeant and tech-savvy super-spy
- Master in the arts of espionage, covert actions, marksmanship and military strategy
- Expert hand-to-hand combatant with advanced ranking in multiple martial-arts disciplines
- Employs a variety of intelligence-gathering capabilities as well as using technologically advanced gadgetry and equipment

A Tale of Two Widows: Part One

igh up in Avengers Tower, Nick Fury, Head of S.H.I.E.L.D., was conducting his weekly briefing with the team.

Suddenly, Fury's comms lit up.

"Hmm," he said to the team, his face worried. "I've just received intel that Black Widow has been spotted in Russia. My sources think she's responsible for stealing some top-secret new technology."

The Avengers looked around at one another, surprised. Black Widow in Russia, committing crimes? Impossible!

Just then, Natasha Romanoff, the Black Widow, strolled into the briefing room, with Hawkeye by her side. "Sorry we're late," she said breezily. "Training ran over."

She looked around at her friends' solemn faces. She could tell immediately that something was off.

Her tone grew serious. "What's going on?" She waited nervously for them to answer. It was beginning to worry her.

The team reluctantly told Natasha there was a Black Widow spotted in Russia who was suspected of stealing cutting-edge tech, and that Fury was headed out there to investigate the sightings.

"I'm going with you," said Natasha.

She wasn't going to let an imposter ruin all the hard work she'd done to overcome her Red Room past.

The Quinjet touched down on a secret airfield outside St Petersburg in Russia. Nobody was supposed to know they were there.

But when Natasha climbed out of the jet ahead of Fury, someone was waiting on the tarmac. The figure was wearing an exact replica of Natasha's Black Widow suit, her face covered with a mask.

Natasha hung back, watching. Hearing the masked figure's voice gave Natasha a strange sense that she somehow knew this person.

A bank of fog rolled in and swirled around the imposter Black Widow.

"Leave," the strange voice said. "Now."

"Get back on your… paper airplane," the figure said, waving a disdainful hand at the Quinjet. "Go back to America."

"Who are you?" demanded Fury. He strode towards the figure. "How did you know we would be here?"

When the fog cleared the imposter was gone. Fury turned to Natasha. "I don't like this," he said.

Natasha didn't like it, either.

Fury and Natasha spent a few days investigating but they didn't get any closer to finding out the identity of the figure in the Black Widow suit or locating the stolen tech.

Then one night, on her way back to a S.H.I.E.L.D. safe house, Natasha heard a soft sound overhead.

Someone was standing on a rooftop above her.

It was the imposter!

"Get out," the masked figure said.

Natasha smiled pleasantly. "Make me," she replied.

The fake Black Widow sprang from the rooftop. Natasha ducked through the air where her head had been. Whoever this was, she was fast… and good. Natasha hissed angrily through her teeth.

Had she met her match? Natasha threw punch after punch and kick after kick.

Her opponent dodged them all easily. Finally, Natasha connected.

POW!

The woman staggered back.

Natasha was panting hard. While the imposter recovered from her punch, Natasha grabbed her phone.

BEEP!

Her phone made a small tone. A distress signal was being sent to Fury. Natasha slipped the phone back into her pocket and launched herself once more at her imposter.

To be continued…

Hawkeye
Clint Barton

Hey! It's Hawk Guy! Ha! Just kidding. A lot of people call him that by mistake. Be we all know that Clint Barton is really Hawkeye, don't we? Don't we? Well, we do now.

- Height: 6' 0"
- Occupation: Avenger
- Master marksman with near-perfect aim
- Utilises a unique bow and a quiver of trick arrows with a variety of effects
- Expert hand-to-hand combatant, athlete and acrobat
- Trained from an early age in the art of archery. His skills earned him the nickname Hawkeye
- Inspired by the deeds of Iron Man and Captain America. He puts his sharpshooting skills to work as a member of the Avengers

Make Way for Widow

He had been paying attention during the mission brief, but couldn't remember. "Um… open sesame?" he whispered.

"Incorrect!" the computer snapped.

WEEEOOO! WEEEOOO! WEEEOOO!

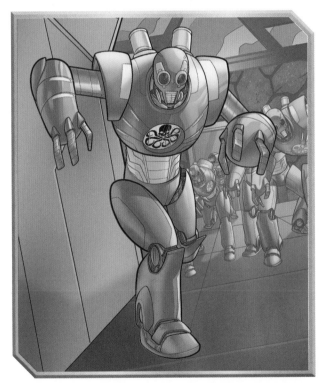

One stormy night, Black Widow and Hawkeye had infiltrated a secret Hydra base. They were after a flash drive that was inside a locked vault. All Hawkeye had to do to open the vault was say the code words. There was just one problem – he had forgotten what they were.

Hawkeye's mistake triggered every alarm in the building.

Moments later, they had been spotted by Hydra's robot guards. They raced for the exit. As they ran, Black Widow and Hawkeye saw rooms filled with strange Hydra experiments.

He was silent for a moment, then said, "Where am I? Who are you? What's going on here?!"

Black Widow was stunned. "Hawkeye… please don't tell me you've lost your memory."

Before Hawkeye could reply, the Hydra robots grabbed them both and threw them into separate jail cells, leaving their weapons in a heap outside the cell doors.

"Come on," said Hawkeye. "We're almost there!"

Black Widow reached the exit first, but as Hawkeye caught up with her, he was knocked on the head by a Hydra guard. Hawkeye fell to the ground with a thud!

"This is bad," said Black Widow, pacing back and forth. Not only were they trapped, she also needed her friend to remember who he was so they could escape from their cells.

"What's your name again?" a confused Hawkeye asked.

"I'm Black Widow," she replied. "You're Hawkeye. We're Avengers." She paused. "You really don't remember anything?"

Hawkeye tried his hardest, but he couldn't remember a single thing about his life as part of Earth's Mightiest Heroes.

Black Widow reminded her partner all about the adventures they'd had as Avengers. She hoped telling him these stories would help his memory recover.

"You were the guy who single-handedly stopped Thanos from destroying the planet," she explained. "That's kind of a big deal."

Hawkeye rubbed his chin. "These are great stories, but they're not ringing any bells. Sorry, lady."

Black Widow was getting very frustrated. "Don't you at least remember me? I'm your partner."

"We argue sometimes," she continued, "but we've always got each other's backs."

Hawkeye looked at Black Widow and squinted. "Hmmm. Now that you mention it, you do look kind of familiar."

Suddenly, Black Widow heard a robot guard's footsteps. They were heading in their direction.

Black Widow climbed up into the ceiling until she was completely out of sight.

"Where did she go?" said the confused robot guard, unlocking the cell door to investigate.

SMACK!
Black Widow dropped down from above and kicked the guard in the face. Its robot head went flying through the air as its body collapsed to the floor, broken beyond repair.

"That takes care of that," said Black Widow, happily.

"You're good at this hero stuff," said Hawkeye, still unable to remember anything about himself.

After leaving the prison far behind them, Black Widow and Hawkeye looked for a way out. They soon came across a tunnel.

"This will take us to the roof," said Black Widow. "There's a jump ship we can use to escape."

"Wow," said an impressed Hawkeye. "You really know your stuff."

They climbed up on to the rooftop to find themselves surrounded by robots once more. "I'm getting a little tired of this," growled Black Widow.

With Hawkeye unable to remember how to use his arrows, Black Widow took on the robots by herself. Using all her strength, she smashed two Hydra robots into one another, destroying them in a burst of sparks.

However, there were so many of them that she knew she needed Hawkeye's help.

"Get it together, Hawkeye!" cried Black Widow. "You're the world's best marksman. It's time you remembered that."

Hawkeye felt a jolt in his brain. His memory had returned at last!

His partner's words were exactly what he needed to hear. "Check this out," he said, as he shot an arrow through a row of robots like a torpedo.

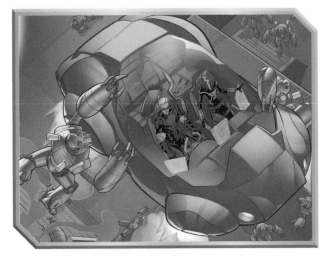

"Welcome back," said Black Widow. "Took you long enough."

Hawkeye ran back to the vault and put in the secret code words. The door unlocked and he grabbed the flash drive.

Hawkeye ran to the jump ship and hopped in. "Time to hit the road," he said. "Get in."

"You sure you know how to fly that thing?" asked Black Widow.

"Trust me," said Hawkeye.

Once inside the ship, the heroes fired up the engine. *KRACKA-THOOM!*

"Smell you later, suckers!" cried Hawkeye, as the ship took off. "Talk about a close call," he added.

"We completed the mission," said Black Widow. "That's what matters."

Hawkeye grinned, then his stomach rumbled. He was starving. "Can we touch down at the nearest taco van?"

"You got it," replied Black Widow with a smile. "Anything for my partner."

"That was disturbing," Fury said to Natasha.

"Agreed," she answered. "Whoever that was, she fought like…" She took a deep breath. "… Like me."

More and more, Natasha couldn't shake the feeling that she knew whoever was behind that mask.

"They're sure that Black Widow is behind the missing tech," Tony told Natasha the next day. He sighed.

"This isn't a great look for the group, Nat," added Steve.

Natasha reeled. "I'm doing my best," she replied shortly.

"We know," said Iron Man, confused by her tone. "We didn't mean—"

Natasha ended the call before he could finish speaking. She'd heard enough. She had to figure out who this person was and clear her name.

Suddenly, the door to her room burst open. Natasha leapt up – the other Black Widow had returned.

"I told you to leave," the imposter grunted between punches.

Natasha threw her attacker into a huge mirror.

CRASH!

It shattered.

The two Widows battled. At the last moment, Natasha reached out and pulled the mask from the woman's face. She gasped in surprise.

"Yelena," she said, shaken. Yelena had been like a little sister to Natasha back in the Red Room where they had both been raised and trained.

Natasha had defected and joined the Avengers, but Yelena had stayed loyal to the Russian government. Apparently she had been made a Black Widow, too.

"Yelena," began Natasha. "It's been so long…"

But Yelena didn't want to be friends. She wanted to fight.

"I have my orders," Yelena said coldly. Natasha dodged her blow.

Yelena kicked at her knee, and Natasha leapt into the air.

"Please…" Natasha started.

But Yelena unleashed a sharp kick that caught Natasha off guard.

Natasha picked herself up. Now she was mad. She flew at Yelena, twisting under her swing to land a sharp blow to her ribs.

"Aah!" yelped Yelena. Natasha ran up the wall and leapt backwards, her feet aiming at Yelena.

But Yelena dodged just in time and kicked out.

The fight seemed to go on and on. Natasha wasn't used to working this hard. Usually she was the best fighter in the room. But Yelena was a Black Widow, too.

Finally, Natasha managed to pin Yelena.

"I'm not leaving," panted Natasha, "until you agree to come home with me."

Now that she knew who this was, Natasha wanted to help Yelena, like she'd been helped so long ago.

Yelena's eyes looked almost sad and longing.

"A Widow never fails," Yelena said, quoting their motto from the Red Room.

Suddenly, Yelena twisted out of Natasha's grip and escaped. But as she disappeared, a small device fell out of her pocket.

Natasha picked it up. It was the tech everyone had been looking for!

"Hurry back to New York, you two," said Tony over the video comms after Fury and Natasha had updated him. "I want to start analysing that tech right away." He grinned at Natasha. "Great work, Nat. You made us look good."

Natasha smiled back. She should have known her teammates would never doubt where her loyalties lay.

As they boarded the Quinjet, Natasha stopped and looked out into the fog.

"Natasha," said Fury, putting a hand on her shoulder. "Let her go. You completed your mission."

Natasha had told Fury what Yelena meant to her.

But Natasha understood that even though her mission was complete, this journey was far from over.

A Widow never fails. Natasha had a feeling Yelena had dropped the device on purpose. For Natasha.

Perhaps her little sister wasn't lost to her, after all.

Either way, Natasha knew she hadn't seen the last of Yelena Belova.

Winter Soldier
James Buchanan 'Bucky' Barnes

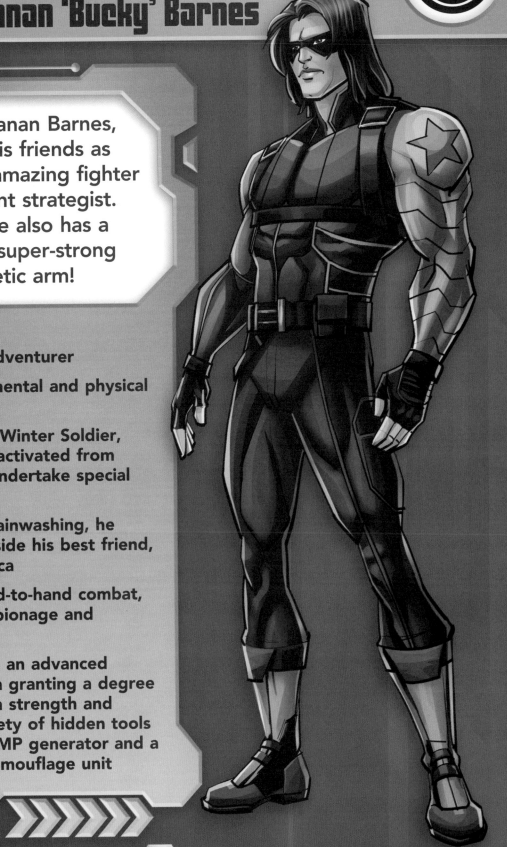

James Buchanan Barnes, known to his friends as 'Bucky', is an amazing fighter and a brilliant strategist. Oh yeah, he also has a super-cool, super-strong cybernetic arm!

- Height: 5' 10"
- Occupation: Adventurer
- Subjected to mental and physical experiments
- Reborn as the Winter Soldier, who could be activated from cryostasis to undertake special missions
- Freed from brainwashing, he now fights beside his best friend, Captain America
- Master of hand-to-hand combat, infiltration, espionage and marksmanship
- Equipped with an advanced cybernetic arm granting a degree of superhuman strength and housing a variety of hidden tools including an EMP generator and a holographic camouflage unit

The Winter Soldier's boots slipped just a little as they slushed into the wet snow on the rooftop. He adjusted his balance but didn't slow down. He was on patrol and was determined to find something interesting to do with his night. As he leapt to the neighbouring roof of a warehouse, he heard a buzzing in his ear.

"Bucky? You there?"

It was Captain America's voice.

"Hey, Cap," answered Winter Soldier. He rolled as he landed on the warehouse's roof.

"GPS has you near Manhattan Bridge," said Captain America over the Avengers comm device in Winter Soldier's ear.

"I always love it when you keep tabs on me," said Winter Soldier, sarcastically. He and Captain America had been partners years ago, back when Winter Soldier was just a kid called Bucky Barnes. Now that he had grown up, Bucky couldn't resist giving his mentor a hard time now and again.

Cap didn't take the bait. Instead, he simply said, "There's a situation. You're about a block away from an inactive top secret S.H.I.E.L.D. base. There's been a break-in."

"Address?" asked Winter Soldier. Bucky didn't mind taking orders, as long as they were from Captain America.

"Underground at the corner of Morris and Second," said Cap. "The facility has been made to look like a standard construction site."

"Wow," said Bucky, as he reached the site. He was impressed. "Now that's a disguise."

Bucky would never have guessed there was more to this building than steel beams and a lift.

"The alarms went off on Sub-basement 2," said Cap. "They've been using the lab there to store a miniature force-field projector.

I've just learned that Taskmaster is trying to get his hands on it. I'm on my way, but it'll take me a few minutes."

"Take your time," whispered Winter Soldier, not wanting to be overheard. "I've been looking for some action tonight anyway."

Winter Soldier turned the volume on his comm unit down low. Then he held his breath for a second. He listened to his surroundings and scanned the high floor of the building with a few cautious glances. Then he moved carefully towards the lift.

He placed the palm of his metal hand against a display panel by the lift's doors. The screen flashed red. Bucky's fingers flexed. A pulse shot from his hand. The screen turned green.

Winter Soldier smiled. His metal arm had saved the day so many times on his missions. Tonight was proving to be no exception.

After a moment or two, the lift opened with a *DING*. Suddenly, a laser blast struck Winter Soldier! Luckily for Bucky, it barely grazed his metal arm.

In front of him, two spinning drones shot off more laser blasts. Winter Soldier jumped into the air. His fingers found the beam above him, and he swung himself up. The drones hummed as they followed.

As the first drone shot up towards him, sending a laser blast that narrowly missed his head, Bucky pounced and grabbed the drone tightly with both hands. It was like trying to hold on to a giant top, but he held on tight. His weight instantly pulled the drone down, crashing it into its companion and knocking it out of the air. Bucky swung towards the nearest beam. He took the drone with him and smashed it into a nearby support pillar. Sparks shot everywhere!

Bucky examined what little of the drone he still held in his hand. This wasn't S.H.I.E.L.D. technology. This belonged to someone else.

He quickly tossed a small capsule up towards the ceiling of the lift, shielding his face as the capsule exploded.

Bucky leapt for the newly formed hole above him just as the platform gave way beneath his feet. His metal hand reached out towards the wall of the lift shaft as he tried to grab on to something… anything…

Suddenly, laughter echoed from inside the lift shaft.

"Sounds like an invitation," Winter Soldier muttered to himself. He stepped into the waiting lift, then pressed the button marked 'Sub-basement 2'.

As the doors closed, Winter Soldier looked up. There was no escape hatch of any kind. He reached into a pouch on his belt.

The lift suddenly lurched. Then it lurched again. Winter Soldier understood what was happening right away. The lift's cables were snapping one by one! Someone had damaged them.

The lift plummeted right past Bucky's intended floor and crashed on Sub-basement 3. The force of the explosion shook the lift shaft. Above the wreckage, a figure hovered on a circular glider.

The man's laughter filled the metal corridor. His helmet lit the room with its fluttering flame: Jack O'Lantern! He was having a great night.

His trap had worked perfectly. The second his drones had detected Winter Soldier, he had begun to damage the lift's cables so they'd break as soon as Winter Soldier stepped inside.

Jack O'Lantern scanned the pile of rubble and steel through his strange flaming helmet.

"What are we looking for?" a voice asked from above him.

Jack O'Lantern glanced up just as one of Winter Soldier's boots struck his pumpkin head. Winter Soldier had been hiding above him in the lift shaft. The force knocked Jack O'Lantern completely off his glider.

The villain hit the ground with a thud, fumbling for words. "How… how did you…?" Too stunned to form a proper sentence, Jack raised his hand and pointed it at Winter Soldier. There was a clicking sound, but nothing else.

Jack O'Lantern's wrist blaster wouldn't fire. It had been damaged in his fall.

"Time to surrender, Pumpkin Spice," said Bucky, with a wry grin.

Jack O'Lantern reached for one of the pumpkin bombs dangling from his belt. He tossed it at Winter Soldier.

Bucky swatted it away, as if it was nothing more than a fly.

The bomb exploded harmlessly against a nearby wall. Winter Soldier smiled wider.

And just like that, Jack O'Lantern wasn't laughing any longer.

"There's no sign of the force-field projector," said Winter-Soldier. "I even checked inside this guy's giant gourd," he continued, smiling down at Jack O'Lantern. The criminal only grunted. "I'll look in the lab next, but—"

Before Winter Soldier could finish his thought, the call dropped. Just then, Bucky heard a rustling of something like wings in the shadows behind him.

"It's worse than you think," a mysterious voice said.

Winter Soldier tightened his fists, ready for another fight.

The night was finally getting interesting.

To be continued...

It was quiet in Sub-basement 3 as Winter Soldier finished tying Jack O'Lantern's restraints.

Suddenly, Bucky's comm unit broke the silence.

"I'm almost there," said the voice of Captain America in his ear. The voice was muffled. There wasn't much reception so far underground.

"You missed the party," said Winter Soldier. "I nabbed Jack O'Lantern here, but I think we still have a problem."

"What's going on?" asked Captain America.

Falcon
Sam Wilson

Not all heroes wear capes – this one wears wings! Sam Wilson, also known as Falcon, patrols the skies to keep everyone safe from all kinds of aliens, super villains and giant, earth-shattering monsters.

- Height: 6' 0"
- Occupation: Avenger
- Inspired by an encounter with Captain America to become a Super Hero
- Wears a sophisticated harness granting high-speed flight and precise aerial manoeuvrability
- Harness can detach and operate autonomously in 'Redwing Mode'
- Superb athlete and hand-to-hand combatant
- Highly intelligent with proficiency in advanced technology

A figure hovered in the darkness above Winter Soldier. The lights in the hallway of the S.H.I.E.L.D. facility had been damaged, causing a flicker that made it hard to see. Bucky steeled himself for battle. Then the man swooped down into the light, his boots padding silently against the metal floor as he landed.

"We need to move fast," said Falcon, leaving the shadows behind. "This way."

Falcon sprinted determinedly towards the stairwell. Without hesitation, Bucky followed, equally ready for action.

As they raced to the laboratory one floor up, Falcon filled Bucky in on what had happened. He felt like he was missing something. Something important…

Falcon had been flying home earlier that evening, ready to turn in. It had been a particularly tiring night of patrol, and Sam Wilson was doing his best to relax and enjoy the rest of the night. The fresh snow falling in the crisp air made that a little easier for him.

That's when he saw the dark cloud moving towards him. At first, Falcon couldn't understand what he was seeing. The cloud was swirling and swaying, as if pulsing with life. As he flew closer, Falcon realised it wasn't a cloud at all. It was a swarm of bats!

Falcon did his best to use his wings as a shield against the sudden swarm. Fortunately, the bats weren't all that interested in him. They seemed to have another target in mind.

Falcon watched to see where they were heading. As if with a single mind, the bats dived towards a nearby construction site.

"What in the world?" said Falcon, under his breath. Then he put his wings to his sides and dived to follow.

As he closed in on the bats, Falcon could see that they were flying straight towards a lift at the centre of the abandoned site. The doors to the shaft were open, as if expecting the winged creatures. Falcon clenched his jaw and dived faster.

He swooped into the empty lift shaft after the bats. The doors were closing, but Falcon managed to make it through before they slammed shut.

Falcon felt like he was diving forever as his eyes adjusted to the dark lift shaft. He realised that he and the bats must be far underground by this point. This empty construction site wasn't what it appeared to be.

Finally, the bats exited through the open doors of a floor marked 'Sub-basement 2'. Falcon slowed his speed and landed just outside the lift. The hallway was completely deserted.

The corridor was lined with glossy metal walls and thick steel doors that were locked tight.

Hi-tech security cameras were mounted on the ceiling, each with a broken lens. Falcon recognised the technology right away. This was a S.H.I.E.L.D. base.

The hallway stretched out in front of the hero. Falcon could see the flutter of wings near its end, and what seemed to be the light of an open door. He hadn't taken more than a few steps forward when two bat-shaped throwing stars shot into his wing. Falcon had no time to react. Suddenly, a much larger bat was headed straight for him!

As Falcon bent backwards to dodge the speeding 'bat', he realised what he was actually facing. It was a glider, one used by a villain he and Captain America had faced many times in the past. A criminal who just happened to be able to control bats.

"When I called for reinforcements, I wasn't expecting anyone human," said a voice from down the corridor.

Falcon's suspicions had been confirmed. "Blackwing," said Sam, as the villain's glider crashed into the wall behind him.

Blackwing reached into his cape and pulled out a battle baton. Without another word, he charged at the hero, his bats leading the way.

Falcon took to the air. There wasn't much room to move around in the tight corridor, but he wasn't in the mood for anything fancy, anyway. Falcon simply flew directly at Blackwing.

Falcon pierced the cloud of bats like a javelin hurtling towards its target. Blackwing's eyes widened as he saw this bullet of a man heading straight for him. The villain tried to dodge the hero, but it was too late. Blackwing was knocked backwards, through the open doorway at the end of the hall and into a glass work surface in the hi-tech S.H.I.E.L.D. laboratory.

Sam was still in motion and flipped forward off the villain.

He was instantly back on his feet.

Blackwing wasn't as graceful. He lay on the ground in a pile of broken computer components. He tried to speak but let out a pitiful groan instead. Then he was completely unconscious.

"And this is where I left him," said Falcon. He and Winter Soldier had burst into that same S.H.I.E.L.D. laboratory on Sub-basement 2. They had made the sprint from the lower floor in seconds.

"You were talking over your comm link earlier about a force-field projector," said Falcon. "I've seen prototypes before, but this guy didn't have anything like that on him." He nodded at Blackwing, lying in a lump in the middle of the room. "Only thing that stood out to me was that empty safe."

"So Jack O'Lantern and Blackwing were just cover?" said Winter Soldier. He bent down and picked up Blackwing's battle baton.

"That's what I'm thinking," said Falcon. "Low-level henchmen to keep us busy."

"Comm's down," said Winter Soldier, tapping his ear. "Cap's on his way, but I don't know when—"

"Wait," interrupted Falcon. "Over there." He pointed to a lone bat, flapping in the corner of the lab. The confused creature flew into the hallway, but in the opposite direction of the lift shaft. "I think there's another way out of there," said Falcon.

Falcon leapt into the air, and Winter Soldier raced after him. They followed the bat into a long, empty tunnel.

Near the end of the tunnel stood a figure dressed in orange and blue. As he turned to face the heroes, Falcon instantly recognised him. It was Taskmaster! He was a villain more dangerous than Blackwing and Jack O'Lantern combined.

In one hand, Taskmaster clutched a shield, similar to that of Captain America. In the other, he held a small device about the size of a remote control. Falcon realised the device Taskmaster was holding was S.H.I.E.L.D.'s missing force-field projector.

"I knew I should've hired more guys," said Taskmaster.

Without taking his eyes off the villain, Falcon spoke to Winter Soldier under his breath. "Go for the button."

Winter Soldier narrowed his eyes. He had worked with Falcon enough times to know exactly what he meant.

As Taskmaster readied his shield to hurl it at the heroes, Winter Soldier threw Blackwing's battle baton.

Winter Soldier had always been an expert marksman. This throw was no exception. Blackwing's battle baton hit the button on the projector just as Falcon flew full speed at Taskmaster. The two heroes had worked with Captain America enough to know what to expect – Bucky went low while Falcon went high.

Taskmaster didn't think twice. He simply launched the shield at the oncoming Falcon. If he had used that second thought, Taskmaster might have realised that the force-field projector had been switched on. But as it was, the shield ricocheted off of the protective energy shield and was reflected right back at him. The blast stunned the villain just as Falcon tackled him off his feet.

The force-field projector fell out of Taskmaster's hand and slid across the floor.

The projector came to a stop at Captain America's boots.

"Guess you didn't need my help," said Cap, as he picked up the device. He pressed the main button on the projector. The force field around Taskmaster instantly shut down.

The villain put his gun on the floor and raised his hands in a gesture of surrender.

"What, you think you're the only Captain America in town?" said Winter Soldier, grinning at Cap. He patted Falcon on the back, and Falcon grinned, too.

The heroes pulled Taskmaster to his feet and began walking him back towards the S.H.I.E.L.D. base. The lights of the hallway were bright above them, but there was hardly a shadow in sight.

Wasp
Hope Van Dyne

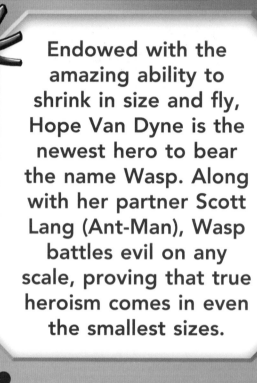

Endowed with the amazing ability to shrink in size and fly, Hope Van Dyne is the newest hero to bear the name Wasp. Along with her partner Scott Lang (Ant-Man), Wasp battles evil on any scale, proving that true heroism comes in even the smallest sizes.

- Height: 5' 4"

- Occupation: Scientist

- When in her shrunken state, can fly at high speeds using insect-like wings

- 'Wasp Stings' discharge powerful electric energy from her hands

The Wonders of Wasp

Hope van Dyne was worried about her dad, Hank Pym. Years leading a double life as the Super Hero, Ant-Man, was taking its toll.

She knew her dad wouldn't give up being Ant-Man unless there was someone who could replace him. And Hope knew exactly who that someone could be. He was Hank's apprentice and his name was Scott Lang.

After Hope told Scott her plan, he agreed to become the new Ant-Man. Now she just needed to convince her dad.

"If Scott is going to be the next Ant-Man," Hank said to his daughter, "then you'll be... Wasp!"

So Scott and Hope became the dynamic Super Hero duo Ant-Man and The Wasp!

One day, Hope and Scott were working in their lab when they received an incoming message from the Avengers. "Hey," said Cap. "We've got something of a situation and think you're the perfect pair for the job.

The pair then hurried out of the lab and flew off to Avengers Tower.

"Here's the plan," instructed Wasp, taking charge. "We need you to neutralise the threat as best as possible, while Ant-Man and I stay here and develop an antidote that will cut Beetle back down to size."

"The Scarlet Beetle has obtained some sort of growth serum that has made him enormous," continued Cap, showing Hope and Scott a string of satellite images. "And not only that, but he seems to be using the serum to create an army of gigantic bugs."

Ant-Man and Wasp had faced Scarlet Beetle before and knew how dangerous he was. "We're on our way," said Wasp.

"Let's get going," finished Wasp, as she and Ant-Man watched the Avengers swoop away. "We've got no time to lose!"

"What are we doing again?" asked Ant-Man.

"We need to make an anti-growth serum," Wasp explained to her friend, as she raced around the Avengers lab, collecting supplies.

Wasp smiled. "Chemistry can be funny that way. We're going to need to go into the field to get it though."

Soon, the serum was assembled and bubbling, but there was one key ingredient still missing.

"Beetle's growth serum!" announced Wasp, suddenly. "We need it to complete the antidote!"

Ant-Man looked confused. "We need the growth serum to finish the anti-growth serum?"

Serum now in place, Ant-Man and Wasp flew off to join the Avengers.

They found the heroes fighting bugs who were all insanely, super-crazily huge!

"Incoming!" shouted Ant-Man, as he dived towards a giant hornet and wrestled it to the ground. "I've got the DNA we need!" he called out to Wasp.

"So, before we join the others," continued Wasp, "let's feed the serum through our gloves so that, with a bit of big-bug DNA, the serum will be complete and – booyah! – we'll be in business."

Wasp helped Ant-Man feed the DNA into the serum in his glove, then her own, and the formula was complete. Immediately, the pair began to spray the serum from their gloves, but the giant bugs were still appearing too fast.

"Beetle is spreading his serum faster than we can spread ours!" said Wasp. "We need to catch him by surprise and stop him." She paused, then said, "I've got an idea!"

Moments later, Ant-Man and Wasp were loaded onto the top of Hawkeye's arrow. "Okay, Hawkeye," said Wasp.

"You'll shoot us off your arrow directly towards Beetle. We'll spray our serum everywhere we possibly can and, this way, he'll never see us coming until we're right in the thick of it." She turned to Ant-Man. "Ready?"

Ant-Man nodded. "Lock and load!"

his face. "You got through my defences. So what? You're going to stop me with… your brains?!" he crowed.

Wasp grinned. "Yeah, kinda," she replied, as she and Ant-Man began to unleash the serum smoke they had created.

"Eat dust, Beetle!" cried Wasp, as she prepared for the final strike. "Or should I say… eat dirt?"

"Here were go!" called Wasp, as Hawkeye fired a well-aimed arrow. She and Ant-Man zoomed towards Beetle and the centre of his insect army. They spread the serum as they flew and were soon in position.

The duo hopped off Hawkeye's arrow at just the right moment and landed in the centre of Beetle's core army.

Beetle saw his two timeless foes and let out a cry of surprise that they'd made it this far. Then, an evil smile spread over

She and Ant-Man blasted Beetle and his army with their serum until they shrunk down, down, down, at last back to their normal size.

As they did so, Ant-Man called upon his ant friends to help Wasp and himself defeat Scarlet Beetle once and for all.

"Noooooo!" cried out Scarlet Beetle, as he watched his chance for world domination disappear.

"We did it!" cried Wasp, high-fiving Ant-Man and thanking the ants who had turned up to help. "Now, let's get back to the lab. I want to bottle up this serum for next time," she added, before flying off.

"Next time?" asked Ant-Man, with a nervous chuckle. "Next time?? Wasp – next time?!?"

Ms. Marvel
Kamala Khan

You already met Captain Marvel, but did you know there's a Ms. Marvel, too? Her name is really Kamala Khan, and she's a high school student living in New Jersey. As it turns out, she's also an Inhuman!

- Height: 5' 4"
- Occupation: Student
- Transformed when the Inhumans released the Terrigen Mist
- Morphogenic abilities, including shapeshifting and the ability to extend her limbs
- Healing factor
- Superhuman speed and strength
- Bioluminescence

"Birds?" asked Hawkeye, confused, as he bent over a pile of loose feathers. Black Widow and Hawkeye were looking for a villain who was reportedly building his own army. They had tracked him to a local pet shop that had just been robbed. "Why would this villain want to steal birds?"

Black Widow frowned as she picked up a big yellow feather. "Something isn't right. Look at the size of this feather." Suddenly, a rustle sounded inside the shop. "Wait, did you hear that?"

SQUAWK!
A giant man-sized bird burst out of the pet shop carrying a cage filled with squawking birds in each hand.

"Oh, what a nice surprise!" the strange bird-man exclaimed. "I finally get to meet the Avengers. I'm sure you've heard of me."

"The Inventor," said Black Widow, narrowing her eyes.

"You know this guy?" asked Hawkeye, as he reached for an arrow.

"Unfortunately," she replied. "He's an evil mutated clone of Thomas Edison and somebody's pet bird."

The Inventor let out an evil laugh. "Well, would you look at the time, I'm just so busy these days with global domination and such. Ta-ta, Avengers!"

With that, the Inventor threw down two strange devices that allowed him to escape deeper into the pet shop with the stolen birds.

"Hawkeye, try to take him down with your arrows," commanded Black Widow, pulling out her electric batons. "I'll corner him."

The heroes took off into the shop, chasing after the super villain. The stolen birds squawked as the Inventor reached the back of the shop. The heroes had him trapped!

Suddenly, the Inventor revealed another much larger gadget and gave an evil smile. "I'm off!"

The villain pressed a bright red button, turning the gadget into a mini jet. With the Inventor at the helm, the jet burst through the ceiling of the shop, and he flew out of sight.

"What just happened?!" asked Hawkeye.

"I don't know, but I do know we need backup," replied Black Widow, turning on her communicator. "Call Bruce Banner," she commanded the device.

"Make sure Thor tags along, too," suggested Hawkeye. "And tell them to keep a low profile. We need to sneak up on this guy."

As Black Widow filled Bruce in on the situation, Thor strolled into the room.

"Hello comrade!" said Thor, joyfully. "I overheard the whole thing, and I've got an idea."

Bruce looked at Thor's outfit. "Low profile?"

Thor smiled. "Yes! And there's someone I'd like you to meet."

"Arghhh!" screamed Kamala Khan, as she slammed her fist against the school building. She had just failed a major biology test. "That super villain kept me up all night. I should have studied."

Only a few people knew that Kamala was the Super Hero Ms. Marvel.

The man quickly removed his tattered hat and coat. Kamala gasped. It was Thor, Prince of Asgard!

Suddenly, the second man let out a roar. As his shirt ripped apart, the Hulk was revealed – so much for keeping a low profile.

"I apologise for approaching you in disguise," said Thor. "We were trying to be discreet. You see, a super villain named the Inventor is here in Jersey City. He's been kidnapping teenagers and turning them into—"

She had the power to stretch, morph and heal. Her fists were powerful, too. Just ask the wall.

"Ms. Marvel," boomed a deep, princely voice. Kamala turned to see two strange men. The one wearing a hat and coat said, "Come with us."

Kamala was suspicious. Who were these guys and how did they know her Super Hero name? Kamala thought there could be only one explanation – they must have been looking for trouble. Her temper flared again.

"All right, let's go, big guy!" she cried.

"Excellent," the man said, cheerfully. "I shall lead the— whoa!"

He yelled in surprise as Kamala threw a punch in his face.

"I'm gonna stop you right there," said Kamala. "This is the last thing I need right now. I should be studying, not chasing after weird villains. If I don't study for my next exam, I'm going to fail biology! Why can't you Avengers just leave me alone!"

She ran down the street, seething with anger.

Kamala knew she had a bad temper. She shouldn't go around yelling at Asgardian warriors, or anyone, like that. But it wasn't her fault that she had powers. What if she didn't want to be a Super Hero?

BRRRING!

Just then, she heard alarms. A pet shop was being robbed! Kamala hung her head. Knowing she had to help, she quickly changed into her Ms. Marvel suit.

"Help! A super villain is robbing my shop!" shouted the owner.

Ms. Marvel saw red. This evil thing was going to regret ever stepping foot in her city. She stretched one of her arms and grabbed the criminal.

She gasped. Was that a... beak?

The creature screeched loudly. "Squawk! Squaaawk!"

"Be quiet!" yelled Ms. Marvel, angrily. The creature yelped in surprise. Just then, Ms. Marvel felt two strong hands grip her arm. Hulk and Thor had arrived.

Kamala released the creature and Hulk took hold of it.

She then took off her mask and fell to her knees. What was she thinking? She could've really hurt someone.

Thor sat down beside her. "You know, we three have a lot in common," he said.

"I doubt it," replied Kamala.

"It's true," said Thor. "I used to have quite the temper, too. And this big green guy used to cause all kinds of problems before he learned to control his temper."

Kamala wiped away a tear. "Really? Because from where I'm sitting, you seem pretty perfect. You're an Avenger."

"Even Avengers aren't perfect," said Thor. "You let your temper get the better of you

today, but it doesn't define who you are. Now, let's go and stop the Inventor."

With that, Kamala picked herself up and took Thor's hand. The two heroes flew off, ready to fight.

CRASH!

Ms. Marvel, Thor and Hulk burst into the Inventor's lair alongside Black Widow and Hawkeye. It was filled with bird-people. The flock attacked in a flurry of feathers and a chorus of cheeps, as the heroes kicked, punched, swung and spun until Ms. Marvel's fists were aching.

"How wonderful! You came," said a shrill voice.

The heroes looked up. It was the Inventor! He was standing on top of some kind of giant robot.

"Welcome to your doom!" he chirped. "Perhaps you're wondering what I am doing here. Well, make yourselves comfortable and I shall tell—"

"You're stealing pet birds and putting their DNA into people you recruited for your villainous bird-army," said Ms. Marvel.

"Oh," mumbled the Inventor, annoyed. "You already know."

"Thor told me on the way over here," said Ms. Marvel. The Asgardian gave a hearty snort. "So, with that out of the way, let's move straight to the showdown."

She enlarged herself until she was as high as the ceiling, grabbed a huge metal machine and smashed it into the Inventor's robot, destroying it completely!

They did it! Ms. Marvel and Thor had defeated the Inventor. But how were they going to fix all of these bird-people?

"Got it," said Ms. Marvel, pushing a big red 'Reverse' button on the Inventor's machine, the Mutator 3000. Suddenly, after a flash of light, the room was full of normal people and exotic birds.

"I've got an idea," said Thor. "Let's go back to Avengers Tower and calm Hulk down. I'm sure Bruce Banner would be happy to tutor you in biology!"

With that, the heroes took off with a cheerful Ms. Marvel by their side.

Loki

Trickster of Asgard

Sometimes it's hard to get along with your sibling. But what would you do if your sibling was the Asgardian Loki, an ace troublemaker if ever there was one? Well, if you're Thor, you constantly try to stop your brother from doing whatever terrible thing it is he's trying to do.

- Height: 6' 4"
- Occupation: Troublemaker
- Raised in Asgard as a foster brother to Thor
- Mischievous trickster
- Member of the virtually immortal Jotun race
- Superhuman strength, speed, endurance and resistance to injury
- Master of reality manipulation, including shapeshifting, mind control and illusion-casting
- Wields a mystical sceptre capable of enhancing his powers

Mischief Maker

Thor and Loki were hurtling home to Asgard. The Avengers had just defeated one of Loki's evil plans. "You've caused enough trouble for one lifetime," said Thor. "You'll be in prison until your trial."

"As you command, dear brother," replied Loki, with a sneer.

The cell could contain his body, but it couldn't keep him from playing his mind games with people.

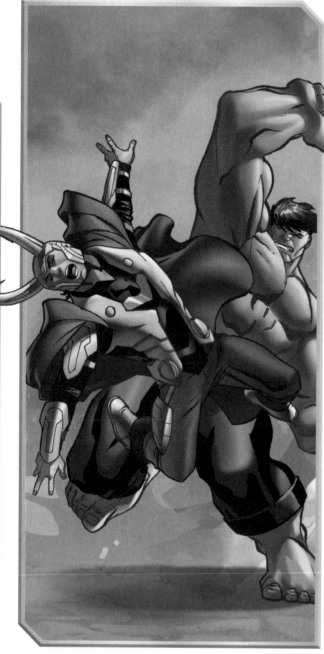

On Earth, Banner suddenly found himself surrounded by vicious warriors. It was Loki's trick, but to Banner, the marauders seemed real. Banner transformed into Hulk, but he was actually attacking peaceful villagers, who were terrified!

Loki had one specific person in mind – Hulk. Loki recalled all the times he'd been on the end of one of Hulk's fierce punches. If he could get inside the green hero's head, he would create lots of trouble for the Avengers. Loki closed his eyes and located Doctor Bruce Banner.

Just as Loki planned, S.H.I.E.L.D. responded to the attack by calling the Avengers. Thor came down to Loki's cell. "I am needed on Earth once more," he said. "Your trial will have to wait until I get back."

Grabbing his hammer, Thor made his way to the Bifrost Bridge to be transported back to Earth. He did not know what happened to cause Hulk to lose his cool, but he would help the Avengers figure it out.

Iron Man, Captain America, Black Widow and Hawkeye were in the middle of a training simulation when they received a report of the attack.

They hurried off in a Quinjet to make sure the big guy did not do any more damage than he had already.

"Don't worry," Iron Man said to the villagers, "we're here to help. Which way did he go?"

The villagers pointed to a path of destruction behind them.

As the heroes hurried to find and stop their friend, Thor arrived. Loki created an illusion of Hulk charging directly at Thor.

The Asgardian prince quickly jumped out of the way. "It is me," Thor said to Hulk, pleadingly. "Your fellow Avenger!"

'Hulk' ignored Thor and charged again. The Asgardian warrior swung his hammer low to trip him, but his hammer went right through the illusion.

"Up to your old tricks again, brother," he cried. "I know what you need."

Thor summoned the Bifrost Bridge and returned to Asgard.

Meanwhile, the other Avengers had found the real Hulk. The green Goliath had run away from the village where he thought he was being attacked. Now, he was surrounded by familiar heroes who all seemed to want to fight him, too.

"Easy there, big fella," said Iron Man. "Nobody has to get hurt."

Then, Loki struck again. He made Hawkeye think that Hulk was about to attack. Hawkeye released his arrow, which whistled through the air and hit Hulk, making him even angrier.

Hulk picked the arrow up and flung it towards Iron Man. He dodged just in time and fired a repulsor blast at Hulk, who was now bearing down on Captain America and Black Widow.

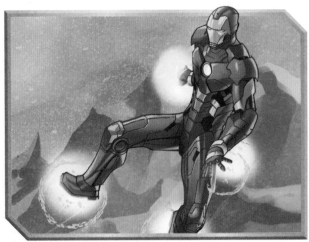

Loki was so caught up in his mischief, he didn't realise Thor had returned until he stormed into his holding cell, grabbed Loki and brought him back to where the other Avengers were battling Hulk.

"Everybody stop fighting!" cried Thor. "Loki is to blame for this mess."

The other Avengers advanced towards Loki. But the trickster used his power to create multiple illusions of himself, so that the heroes could not tell which was the real one.

Suddenly, Hulk swung his arm in a wide arc until he hit the real Loki, who crumpled to the ground. "No more tricks!" said Hulk, angrily.

"Your fun is over," agreed Thor. "It's back to prison for you, brother."

Loki was locked up, once again, on Asgard. After helping rebuild the village Hulk had rampaged through, the Avengers settled in to enjoy their victory.

Monkey Business

One sunny day, Captain Marvel was flying over the New York City skyline when she felt her comms buzz. The Super Hero knew exactly who was radioing in.

"Danvers, you're late with the package!"

Nick Fury was not known for being patient. But before she could reassure Fury she would be at Avengers Tower soon, a voice cut through Carol's thoughts.

"Aaahh! Help me!"

Captain Marvel recognised the sound of distress all too well. In an instant, she changed course and flew towards the source of the worried cries.

Captain Marvel swooped in just in time to catch a little girl who was about to fall off the monkey bars.

"Well, that was a close one!" exclaimed Captain Marvel, as she helped the girl to her feet.

"Thanks for saving me," the little girl said.

"She only had to save you because you're too scaredy-cat to finish the monkey bars!"

Captain Marvel looked around to see a group of kids poking fun at the little girl.

"It's not cool to make fun of someone for falling," Captain Marvel told the kids. "Everybody stumbles now and then." She helped lift the girl back onto the monkey bars'

ladder. "Sometimes the bravest thing a person can do is get back up after they fall. Trust me, I may be a Super Hero and I may be strong, but I've been outsmarted before."

She told the children about the harrowing past few days: the Asgardian trickster, Loki, had tried to steal a magical gem from a faraway planet.

"He used the explosive rocks on the planet to attack me. I thought I had lost. But then, when I wasn't expecting it, I found the strength inside me to get back up."

"And you took something that I want back... now!" boomed a villainous voice.

Captain Marvel froze. She would recognise that voice anywhere.

"Loki!" she cried. "Show yourself!"

"Try looking behind you!" said Loki, chuckling.

Captain Marvel turned around and couldn't believe what she saw. Right before her eyes, the little girl had disappeared in a swirl of smoke, and now swinging from the monkey bars was none other than Loki himself!

"Loki!" exclaimed Captain Marvel. "It was you all along?"

"Yes, I am here to reclaim what's mine," replied Loki. "You may be strong, but your one disadvantage is that you are compelled to protect the weak."

Without warning, Loki raised his sceptre and fired a powerful energy beam.

"Run, kids!" yelled Captain Marvel, covering the children from Loki's attack.

The children ran in panic, but one of them tripped and fell to the ground.

"It's okay, Captain Marvel," said Nina, bravely. "I may have fallen..." Nina quickly grabbed the gem and got to her feet, "... but I can always get back up!"

"Nina!" her friends called after her.

Captain Marvel turned to make sure Nina was okay, and at that moment, Loki's blast hit her bag, and the gem went flying.

Loki saw his opportunity as Captain Marvel ran to Nina. "Ha! Just as I predicted, you are a sucker for anyone in distress!"

She threw the gem towards Captain Marvel, who caught it in midair as she leapt acrobatically after Loki, knocking him backwards.

"Wow, that was so brave!" said Captain Marvel, after she had secured Loki and it was safe for the other kids to return.

"I remembered what you said about never staying down," smiled Nina, shyly, "and how we all have an inner strength when things get tough."

"Nice job," said Captain Marvel. Suddenly, her comms buzzed again. "I'm on my way, Fury, and I've got a two-for-one special for you today!"

"Hail Hydra!" cried Red Skull. Along with Arnim Zola and Baron Zemo, Red Skull led the forces of Hydra against the Avengers along with their army of loyal goons. Spoiler alert! They always lost!

- Terrorist Organisation boasting some of the most evil villains in history among its ranks
- In existence since World War 2
- Founded by Wolfgang Von Strucker
- Opposing force to S.H.I.E.L.D.
- Current members include Baron Strucker, Red Skull, Madame Hydra and Arnim Zola

M.O.D.O.K.
Scientist Supreme

- Height: 12' 0"
- Occupation: Would-be conqueror
- Originally a man named George Tarleton, a skilled technician
- Subjected to experiments that resulted in superhuman intelligence and psionic powers
- Refers to himself as 'Scientist Supreme'
- His large cranium is in a hoverchair which magnifies his psionic abilities

M.O.D.O.K. has superhuman intelligence as a result of an evil genetic experiment. He also has a really, really, and we mean really, big head.

A New Squirrel in Town

The girl who was headed to Avengers Tower with a platter of cookies didn't look like anything special. Well, that's not quite true. She looked like a squirrel. But the point is, she didn't look like an especially powerful squirrel. Even though she was. In fact, she was the Unbeatable Squirrel Girl!

When the girl reached Avengers Tower, she found the heroes standing outside.

"A Girl Scout!" cried Thor.

"It's Squirrel Girl, actually," replied the girl. "And I'm here to join the Avengers. I made cookies. See?"

"Doreen Green," said Iron Man, recognising her. "Thor, this is no Girl Scout. Doreen has the powers of a squirrel."

Squirrel Girl nodded eagerly as Thor took a cookie. "Yep! And I—"

BRRRING!

Suddenly, Bruce Banner's Danger Detector went off.

"My readings are showing a mysterious fog taking over the city," said Banner.

"Avengers, assemble!" commanded Captain America.

The Avengers took off, with Squirrel Girl hot on their heels.

"No way, Girl Squirrel!" shouted back Iron Man.

"It's Squirrel Girl, Man Iron," she corrected. "And I want to help!"

Bruce Banner took Squirrel Girl to one side. "Look, I'm sorry, Doreen, but you aren't battle-tested," he said. "Maybe you'll be ready one day, but not today."

"But, but..." stuttered Squirrel Girl sadly.

Banner shook his head, and said sympathetically, "You aren't safe here, Doreen. Go home."

Then, with a huge roar, he turned into the Hulk and joined the other Super Heroes.

Squirrel Girl was left all alone.

"I know I can do it," she said.

Why wouldn't the Avengers take a chance on her? Her shoulders slumped and her heart sank.

It wasn't long until Doreen reached the thick, white fog. It was so dense, she could barely see.

"Something isn't right here," said Squirrel Girl. "This fog seems... unnatural. What's causing it? I need to get a better look."

But you can't keep a good squirrel down. Squirrel Girl knew she could be a great Super Hero. "Let's do this thingy," she said, chucking the cookies in the bin.

With the agility of a super-powered squirrel, she launched herself onto the side of a skyscraper. Up, up, up she climbed, until she was above the fog.

Meanwhile, in the middle of the fog, the Avengers were busy saving the day. Iron Man and Falcon swooped through the air while shouting orders down below.

Captain America and Black Widow protected civilians. Hulk picked up cars and placed them in parking spots like they were toys. Thor stood at the centre of the street, trying to stop the fog with his hammer. Lightning and thunder erupted from his mighty weapon into the sky. But the harder he tried, the thicker the fog became.

Using her enhanced squirrel-vision, Squirrel Girl gazed out over the streets of Manhattan.

"Now, if I was an evil weatherwoman, where would I be…?"

Bingo! The fog had cleared enough for Squirrel Girl to see masked men running into a shop.

"Gross. Who wears green to a robbery and— O.M.G.! It's Hydra."

Squirrel Girl had read about these guys. They tried to destroy the city with a destruction ray.

"This is big," said Squirrel Girl, quietly. "I'm going to need some help."

She jumped off the roof of the skyscraper and began to leap nimbly from building to building.

She moved through New York City like a squirrel in the treetops. As she went, she emitted her chittering squirrel call.

Every squirrel in Manhattan heard it and came running.

By the time Squirrel Girl reached the building Hydra was robbing, a huge scurry of squirrels had joined her.

"A jewellery shop!" said Squirrel Girl to her furry friends. She straightened and flashed a giant grin. "Squirrels… assemble!"

The squirrels looked around, confused. Squirrel Girl scrunched her face. "Sorry. That sounded a lot cooler in my head."

Squirrel Girl marched into the jewellery shop.

"Halt!" she yelled.

The Hydra goons stopped in their tracks.

"That's… a lot of squirrels," one of them said, worriedly.

"You better believe it," said Squirrel Girl. "Get 'em, guys!"

Squirrel Girl and her army of squirrels attacked.

The fight was soon over. As Squirrel Girl was tying up the villains, she stood on a weird gadget, crushing it under her foot.

"A weather machine!" cried Squirrel Girl. "I knew it! You guys created the fog. But what were you stealing…?"

Cautiously, she made her way further into the shop.

"Wow!" Her voice dropped to a whisper. "Tippy-Toe, go get the Avengers."

A short while later, the Avengers came running into the jewellery shop.

"Where is Squirrel Girl?" asked Iron Man.

"In here, guys!" cried Squirrel Girl, cheerfully. She was splashing around in an enormous pile of sparkly diamonds!

Iron Man snapped his metal fingers. "The fog was a diversion. Hydra needed these diamonds for their new destruction ray!"

"They would have succeeded, too," said Cap, "if it wasn't for Squirrel Girl."

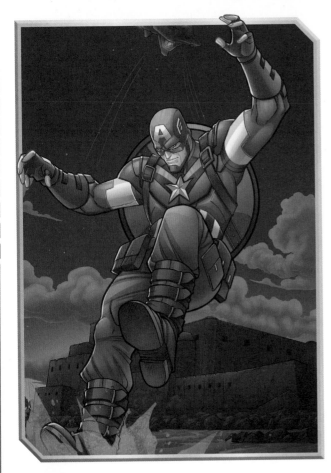

Since he had teamed up with the Avengers, Captain America hadn't been on a solo mission in a very long time. He knew he could hold his own in battle, but this mission sounded… challenging. Cap was nervous, but he knew he had to be brave.

Captain America soon arrived at the island closest to where the cargo ship disappeared. He jumped out of his Quinjet and splashed into the water.

Captain America jogged up the beach towards a towering fortress. All he could hear were the crashing waves and swaying trees.

PEW! PEW! PEW!

Suddenly, the beach lit up with hundreds of bright green blasts, all intended for Captain America.

Captain America was at Avengers Tower. His boss, Nick Fury, had a new mission for the Super-Soldier.

"A massive cargo ship carrying hi-tech battle suits vanished on its route somewhere in the Caribbean Sea," explained Fury.

Cap grabbed his trusty vibranium shield and headed to the roof where his Quinjet was waiting for him. It was time for a trip to the Caribbean.

The powerful blasts knocked Cap to the ground. Then, through the dust and rubble, he spotted a strange shape in the distance…

It was M.O.D.O.K. – a genetically engineered, super-intelligent being who wanted to conquer the world.

This villain was the one who had stolen the battle suits, and he was somehow making the local population of monkeys control them.

Inside the fortress, Captain America sat on the floor. Both his hands and feet were shackled. His trusty shield was nowhere in sight and the barred cell and windows cut off any hope for escape.

M.O.D.O.K. laughed outside Cap's cell. "Now you can watch as I take over the world with my new army!" he said.

"Very original," said Cap. "But how are a few captive monkeys going to help you?"

"I wouldn't say a few," replied M.O.D.O.K., laughing.

M.O.D.O.K. flew out of the fortress to hover outside Cap's cell window. When the hero sat up to look, his eyes widened at the massive army of mechanical primates, all inside the stolen state-of-the-art battle suits.

Captain America knew he needed to fight back!

When his monkey guard walked past, an idea came to him.

The hero slammed his metal cuffs against the iron bars of the cell. The vibrations made the cyborg monkey angry. In a fit of rage, it broke open the cell and threw itself at Captain America.

Cap moved out of the way as the cyborg grabbed his chains, twisting and breaking them into pieces.

Cap vaulted through the cell opening and bent the bars back into shape, trapping the cyborg inside.

He then found his shield, but froze when a giant cyborg hand grabbed him by the shoulder.

In an instant, Cap was under attack by a group of cyborg monkeys! Captain America punched one cyborg and the battle suit exploded.

A frightened monkey scurried out. Suddenly, Cap remembered the monkeys were captives, just like he was.

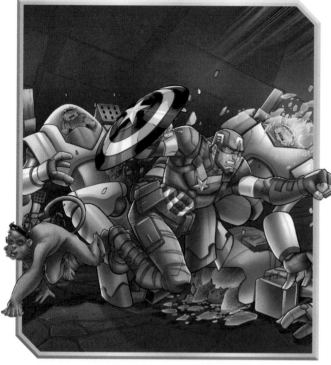

Outside the fortress was another matter. M.O.D.O.K. still had a large army of cyborgs, but if Cap could destroy M.O.D.O.K.'s chair, he knew the signal controlling the monkeys would be stopped.

He was the only hope they had if they were to be free from M.O.D.O.K.'s control.

So, the Avenger destroyed every battle suit he could find inside the fortress, freeing the monkeys as he did so.

So, Cap raced outside and headed towards M.O.D.O.K., intent on stopping his foe.

M.O.D.O.K. gasped when he saw the hero. "Cyborgs, attack!" he cried.

But Captain America was too quick, and before the cyborgs could stop him, he threw his shield at M.O.D.O.K.'s chair, damaging it.

The villain was forced to escape from the island.

The monkeys were now free from M.O.D.O.K.'s mind control.

Captain America helped to release the remaining monkeys and, one by one, they scurried off, happy to be free.

As Cap watched the sunrise, he felt good. Despite being on his own, his courage and determination had helped save the day.

Back on the Quinjet, Captain America signalled Avengers Tower.

"All done?" asked Nick Fury.

"Mission accomplished," replied Captain America.

Ultron
Evil Sentient Robot

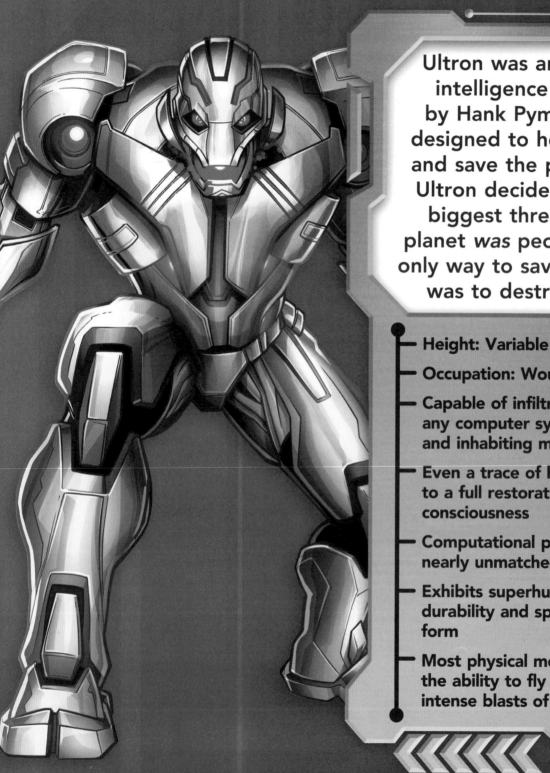

Ultron was an artificial intelligence created by Hank Pym. He was designed to help people and save the planet. But Ultron decided that the biggest threat to the planet *was* people, so the only way to save the world was to destroy them!

- Height: Variable
- Occupation: Would-be conqueror
- Capable of infiltrating virtually any computer system or network and inhabiting mechanical bodies
- Even a trace of his code leads to a full restoration of his consciousness
- Computational prowess is nearly unmatched
- Exhibits superhuman strength, durability and speed in robot form
- Most physical models possess the ability to fly and project intense blasts of energy

Ultron Goes Viral

The Avengers were gathered on the roof of Avengers Tower. Alarms were blaring around them.

"Something unspeakable has happened," Iron Man informed them. "The internet is down!"

"Oh, no!" gasped Black Widow. "All vital Earth systems use the Internet. The electric grid, hospitals, you name it."

Captain America stepped forward. "While the rest of you see what you can do to help, Iron Man and I will find out who is behind this cyber crime."

"Way ahead of you, Cap," said Iron Man. "JARVIS has discovered the culprit – Ultron!

It looks like that evil robot has released a virus into the network."

"I think we might need a little extra help on this one," said Captain America. "We need Captain Marvel."

"Great idea," said Iron Man. He knew Captain Marvel would be their best chance of taking down the robotic menace.

"Everything's a mess," she said. "We need to put a stop to Ultron's virus before he does any permanent damage. Meet me at Alpha Flight Headquarters."

Then, she launched herself into the sky.

The three heroes soared through the air and soon arrived at Alpha Flight HQ. The place was buzzing with activity.

Without wasting another second, Captain America and Iron Man headed off to Captain Marvel's home. She lived in the Statue of Liberty's crown.

When they arrived, Captain Marvel was waiting for them. She already knew about Ultron's scheme.

"Gonzalez!" she said. "Get an encrypted pipeline. O'Connell, initiate offensive network protocol 616."

Soon, a mass of code was scrolling across the many screens within the base.

"Their systems don't appear to be down," said Captain America.

"They must have bypassed the traditional network systems," replied Iron Man.

The two Avengers watched in admiration as Captain Marvel began issuing orders.

"It's digital warfare," explained Iron Man. "She's hunting Ultron's virus."

He turned to Captain Marvel. "He'll know where this is coming from," he warned. "Ultron will come and shut us down."

"Let him come," smiled Captain Marvel.

At that very moment… *BOOM!*

Ultron exploded through the wall behind Super-Soldier Captain America.

"How cute," he snarled, grabbing Cap's shield. "Iron Man and Captain America think they can foil my plot to destroy human civilisation."

Iron Man began to laugh. "You've never met Captain Marvel, have you?"

Ultron turned on Captain Marvel and sneered. "I'll soon destroy this puny human woman."

Captain America hit Ultron with a mighty punch, but Ultron was too powerful. He tossed Captain America to one side, then turned on Iron Man.

"Give up, puny humans. Nobody can protect humanity now," taunted Ultron.

"I'm only half-human," said Captain Marvel, swinging a well-aimed punch at the cyber pest's face.

Ultron tackled Captain Marvel to the ground and the pair crashed around Alpha Flight Headquarters in furious, deadly combat.

In the background, the computers whirred with activity. Then… *BING!* They announced that their job was done.

Ultron's virus had been destroyed.

"There you go," smiled Captain Marvel. "Your virus is toast, Ultron, and so are you."

She threw an almighty punch that catapulted Ultron out through the wall and hurled him into outer space!

"Ultron never stood a chance against you," Captain America said to Captain Marvel.

"Nope," replied Captain Marvel, confidently.

Iron Man removed his mask and gave Captain Marvel a high-five. "The internet's back up and Ultron's out of our hair. Sorry, Cap, but it looks like the Avengers have a new Captain!"

Thanos
Titan

Thanos is the most powerful villain of them all. He has been searching the galaxy for the Infinity Stones. Each of the six Stones has a special property. If Thanos gets them all, he will become an unstoppable force of evil!

- Height: 6' 7"
- Occupation: Galactic conqueror
- Strength, durability and stamina that surpasses that of nearly any mortal being
- Can absorb and project enormous quantities of cosmic energy
- Can manipulate matter on an atomic level
- Genius in almost all known sciences, far exceeding the limits of human understanding
- Master strategist and military leader

The Avengers quickly headed there before the villain caused too much trouble.

The Super Heroes found Thanos holding the gem and four other similar-looking stones.

Ｏne day, Nick Fury and the Avengers were having an emergency meeting. A mysterious gem they had recently recovered had gone missing.

"The gem is one of several Infinity Stones," explained Fury. "And I know who took it. His name is Thanos, and he's just been spotted in Central Park."

Thanos placed each of the gems into fitted slots in the gauntlet he was wearing. "Behold, the Infinity Gauntlet!" he cried, triumphantly.

Thanos thrust his fist out and shot an energy beam at Captain America. But Cap raised his shield and deflected the blast towards Thanos, who suddenly fell back.

Taking advantage of Thanos's weakened position, the Avengers encroached from all sides, ready to attack.

Thanos looked around and, seeing he was surrounded, laughed. "I underestimated you Avengers," he said. "But I will see you again very soon."

In a flash of light, he teleported away.

The Avengers assembled on the Helicarrier, S.H.I.E.L.D.'s flying base, to determine a plan for stopping Thanos. Nick Fury was waiting for them.

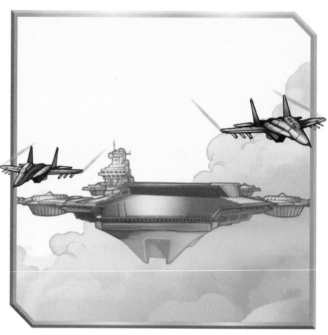

"Thanos clearly wants that last Infinity Stone," said Fury. He explained that wherever the final gem was, Thanos would be there, too.

"The last report of an energy event that might come close was back in the Arctic Tundra," said Iron Man. "Anybody up for some skiing?"

The Avengers called Thor back from Asgard where he'd been guarding Loki and, now a complete team, headed off to the Arctic Tundra in search of Thanos.

It wasn't long before they found him.

Hulk attacked Thanos, smashing his fists into the frozen ground.

Thor threw his hammer at Thanos, who easily deflected it away.

Iron Man then used his thrusters to ram into Thanos.

Black Widow launched herself at Thanos, but he deflected her blows.

Hawkeye even shot a glowing power arrow, but it had no effect.

The Avengers had to find a way to disable the Infinity Gauntlet if they had any chance of beating Thanos.

As Hulk threw himself at Thanos once more, Captain America had an idea.

"Individually, he's too strong for us," he said, "but what if we combined our powers?"

The Avengers agreed. Thor raised his hammer and called down the power of lightning to infuse Captain America's shield.

The gauntlet fell, causing an explosion. Black Widow grabbed the fallen Stones, while Hulk smashed what was left of the gauntlet. Thanos was defeated! But before they could get him, he disappeared.

Iron Man combined Hawkeye's arrows and Black Widow's bracelets to transfer the power of his arc reactor to the shield also.

Iron Man turned to Hulk. "Okay big guy, you're up!"

Hulk took Captain America's energy-infused shield and hurled it towards Thanos, aiming for the Infinity Gauntlet on the super villain's raised fist.

Thanos was still at large, but the Avengers had won. They handed the Infinity Stones to S.H.I.E.L.D. for safekeeping. Thanos would be back, but the Avengers would be ready for him, and for any threat against Earth. After all, they were the mightiest team of heroes in the universe!

Captain America
Sam Wilson

When the world found itself without a Captain America, the question was asked, "Who will wield the shield?" The answer came in the form of Steve Rogers's longtime friend, Sam Wilson – better known as the high-flying Falcon! Though the legendary mantle was a tremendous responsibility, Wilson displayed the same honour, devotion and heroism as his stalwart predecessor, while also carving out his own unique legacy as the new Captain America.

- Height: 6' 0"
- Occupation: Avenger
- Superb athlete and highly trained hand-to-hand fighter
- Equipped with virtually indestructible vibranium shield
- Wears a sophisticated winged harness, granting high-speed flight and precise aerial manoeuvrability
- Harness can detach and operate autonomously in 'Redwing Mode'.

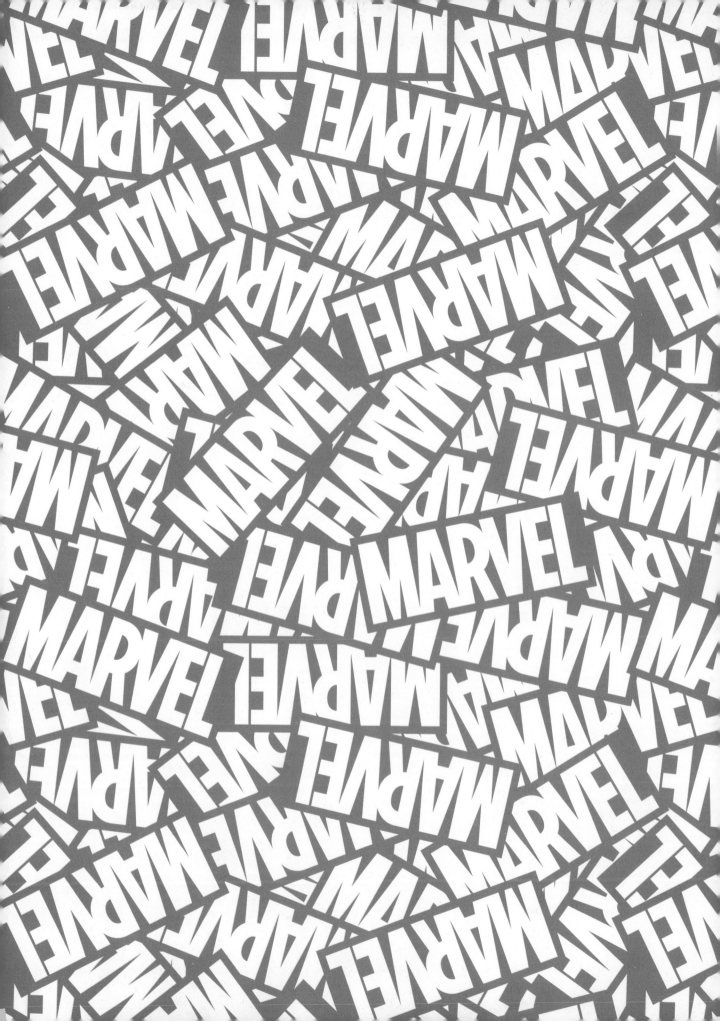